HIS FATHER'S MURDERER

Tell Sackett went into the darkness near the trees. He moved among the spruce, keeping low to the ground.

A voice spoke very low. "Have you found the gold?"

There was a chill along his back. "You killed my father," Tell said.

"He was a good man. I did not wish to do it, but he had my gold."

"The Frenchmen mined the gold. They buried it. They sold their claim to it with Louisiana. It was anybody's gold."

"You will not have it. I will kill you all."

Bantam Books by Louis L'Amour
Ask your bookseller for the books you have missed

BORDEN CHANTRY
BRIONNE
THE BROKEN GUN
THE BURNING HILLS
THE CALIFORNIOS
CALLAGHEN
CATLOW
CHANCY
CONAGHER
DARK CANYON
DOWN THE LONG HILLS
THE EMPTY LAND
FALLON
THE FERGUSON RIFLE
THE FIRST FAST DRAW
FLINT
GUNS OF THE TIMBER-
 LANDS
HANGING WOMAN
 CREEK
THE HIGH GRADERS
HIGH LONESOME
HOW THE WEST WAS
 WON
THE KEY-LOCK MAN
KID RODELO
KILLOE
KILRONE
KIOWA TRAIL
THE MAN CALLED
 NOON
THE MAN FROM
 SKIBBEREEN
MATAGORDA
THE MOUNTAIN VALLEY
 WAR
NORTH TO THE RAILS
OVER ON THE DRY SIDE
THE PROVING TRAIL

THE QUICK AND THE
 DEAD
RADIGAN
REILLY'S LUCK
THE RIDER OF LOST
 CREEK
RIVERS WEST
SHALAKO
SITKA
TAGGART
TUCKER
UNDER THE SWEET-
 WATER RIM
WAR PARTY
WESTWARD THE TIDE
WHERE THE LONG
 GRASS BLOWS
   Sackett Titles by
   Louis L'Amour
 1. SACKETT'S LAND
 2. TO THE FAR BLUE
   MOUNTAINS
 3. THE DAY-
   BREAKERS
 4. SACKETT
 5. LANDO
 6. MOJAVE CROSSING
 7. THE SACKETT
   BRAND
 8. THE LONELY MEN
 9. TREASURE
   MOUNTAIN
10. MUSTANG MAN
11. GALLOWAY
12. THE SKY-LINERS
13. THE MAN FROM
   THE BROKEN HILLS
14. RIDE THE DARK
   TRAIL

LOUIS L'AMOUR
TREASURE MOUNTAIN

TREASURE MOUNTAIN

A Bantam Book / October 1972

2nd printing ...... October 1972   7th printing .. November 1975
3rd printing .... March 1973   8th printing .. November 1976
4th printing .... March 1974   9th printing .... March 1977
5th printing .. November 1974   10th printing .... July 1977
6th printing .... July 1975 11th printing .... April 1978
           12th printing .... January 1979

ISBN 0-553-12827-2

Published simultaneously in the United States and Canada

Bantam Books are published by Bantam Books, Inc. Its trade-
mark, consisting of the words "Bantam Books" and the por-
trayal of a bantam, is Registered in U.S. Patent and Trademark
Office and in other countries. Marca Registrada. Bantam
Books, Inc., 666 Fifth Avenue, New York, New York 10019.

CHAPTER I

"To kill a man, my dear, is not always to make an end of him." The statement was made by Andre Baston.

"But after twenty years? *Twenty years?*" said the woman.

"A lifetime to you, Fanny, but only yesterday to a man like your Uncle Philip."

"But how could anyone *know?* It all happened so long ago, and so far away!"

"Nevertheless, a man is here in New Orleans and he is asking questions. His name is Sackett."

"What?"

"Orrin Sackett. He is an attorney, a lawyer. He has the same name as the man who went to the western mountains with Pierre."

Fanny Baston was small, slender, voluptuous, and beautiful. Her shoulders were soft and amazingly white, her lips were warm and a little full, and her eyes were large.

She shrugged. "What difference can it make? Let him ask his questions. We simply know nothing. Who is left who could possibly know anything?"

Andre scowled. "I do not know. Nobody, perhaps. But I do not like him asking questions. If Philip ever found out . . ."

"It would be the end," Paul said. "The end. He would cut us off, leave us nothing."

"You, perhaps," Fanny said to Andre. "But I was a baby. Not five years old. And Paul, you were not even in your teens. We had nothing to do with it."

"Do you think that would matter?" said Paul. "Uncle Philip only needs an excuse to cut us all off. You too. You aren't exactly his pride and joy, you know."

"Then," she leaned forward, dusting the ash of her small cigar into a saucer, "kill him. Kill this Orrin Sack-

1

ett and drop him in the bayou before he can even be connected to us. Kill him at once."

Andre was no longer surprised at anything his niece said. "You have an idea?"

"Do it yourself, Andre. He would not be the first." She looked up at him and smiled. "Why not? Find an excuse, challenge him. There is not a better shot in New Orleans, and as for a rapier . . . how many men have you killed, Andre? In duels, I mean?"

"Twelve," he replied. "You have a point. It might be the answer."

"You are too bloody," Paul objected. "If you want him killed, there are other ways. We might get him into one of the concert-saloons—the Buffalo Bill House, for example. Williams would take care of him for us."

"No." Fanny spoke sharply. "No, Paul. If there is killing to be done, the fewer who know the better. And nobody outside the family."

"She's right," Andre said, "but this is all so premature. This Orrin Sackett cannot know anything. Pierre was obviously French, obviously from Louisiana. He brought Sackett back here to outfit before we started west, but Sackett never left the river front. I don't know what stirred this up, but all we have to do is sit quietly and allow it to pass. If he gets close then we can act." He shrugged, looking down at the tip of his cigar. "After all, New Orleans may take care of him without our help. He would not be the first."

"Have you seen him?" Fanny asked.

"Yes. He's a big man, nearly as big as I am. Perhaps even as big. He's a good-looking fellow, dresses well, seems to know his way around."

Paul looked up. "Andre, wasn't there some disturbance down on the waterfront a few years back? Some trouble involving some Sacketts?"

"I believe you are right, Paul. I do recall something of the kind. An attempt was made to rob one of them and there was a fight—quite a bloody one."

"That could be the answer, Uncle Andre," Fanny suggested. "A Sackett returns . . . a revenge killing."

She was right, of course. It was a simple, logical method if it became necessary. He would make a few inquiries. If any of the old crowd were around he might just drop a word here and there. Anyway, this was all over nothing. This Sackett knew nothing, could know nothing.

A thought suddenly occurred to him. He still had the map. He had kept it, believing it held a clue to the treasure.

None of them knew he had it, for he had never mentioned it to anyone. After all, when one holds the only clue to the location of thirty million in gold one does not talk about it. The stuff was there. He had taken the time to look up the old reports turned into the government those many years ago, and of course, there was mention of the gold the French army had mined— *thirty millions!*

He had been thinking of going back to look for that gold, and this was probably the time. He was forty years old now, stronger and more able than ever. He must think about the future, and he had little faith in what Philip might leave them. Philip liked none of them too well, and with good reason.

What did Sackett *know?*

Orrin Sackett, standing before his mirror in the Saint Charles Hotel, combed his hair carefully, set his cravat in place, and left his room. At the head of the stairs he paused momentarily and touched his left side lightly. The Smith and Wesson Russian he carried was resting easily. No trouble was expected, but habit remains with a man.

So far the trip had netted him exactly nothing. He had doubted from the first that they would uncover anything. New Orleans was a big city. Twenty years had passed, and the clues he had were slight. Still, if it would please ma there was no effort he would not make.

After all, what information did he have? Twenty years ago a man of strong French accent wanted to make a trip to a certain place in the western mountains. That implied that he had made a previous trip or that he had knowledge of someone who had made such a trip.

Pa had been asked to guide this Frenchman, and the

trip was expected to last but a few months—time to get there and return.

What would take a man to lonely mountains at the risk of being killed by Indians? Furs? To trap furs a man had to remain the winter through. A mine? Perhaps. He might wish to ascertain if the mine was worth development. Yet . . , wasn't it more likely that he knew of gold already mined?

Or thought he did?

When Orrin added up all the information he had, he was looking for a Frenchman, probably from Louisiana, who had some previous connection, direct or indirect, with someone who had been to the western mountains.

Flimsy as that was, it did much to clear the field, for not many Frenchmen had gone west from Louisiana. From Canada . . . yes. Of course, France had controlled all of Louisiana for a time, and, during the period of the Mississippi Bubble and John Law, great efforts had been made to find gold and silver. Law had promised his investors wealth, and he made every effort to discover it—or indications of it.

This Frenchman had not wanted a large party. Yet, it was unlikely that they had actually gone alone.

Hence one of the party might have returned, or there might be a relative who knew something about the affair. The trouble was he had no starting point. Yet, the simplest way was often the best, and that meant checking the obvious sources—in this case, government records of mines, claims, and exploring expeditions in the back country.

Another way, equally simple, was to meet some of the older citizens and start them recalling their youth. It sometimes required patience, but he had an interest in such things and could afford a few days. Or he could get some discussion started of the John Law period—the most likely time for any mineral exploration.

Bienville, during his governorship, had wasted little time searching for nonexistent minerals. His had been a more practical, down-to-earth approach, and, had he been let alone to proceed as he wished, the colony might have been successful long before it was.

At dinner Orrin sat quietly and alone, listening to the

idle talk around him and enjoying the lights and music. He had always enjoyed dining alone, for it gave him time to think as well as to absorb the atmosphere around him. And tonight the dining room was filled with attractive, beautifully gowned women and handsomely dressed men.

The two tables closest to his were occupied: one of them by a group of people of his own age or younger, the other by a very handsome older couple, a distinguished-looking man with a beautiful woman, her hair almost white, her eyes remarkably youthful.

He ordered his meal when the waiter appeared. "And the wine, sir?"

"Châteauneuf-du-Pape," he said quietly.

The older gentleman turned his head and glanced at him. Their eyes met, and Orrin smiled. "An excellent wine, sir," the man said.

"Thank you. Anything less would not fit the surroundings."

"You are a stranger here?"

"I have been here more than once. But this is the first opportunity I have had to relax in a long while." Orrin watched the waiter open his wine, tasted it, then said to the old man, "I am interested in some mining claims in the San Juan Mountains in Colorado. I have heard rumors to the effect that people from New Orleans located mines in that area."

The old man smiled. "I doubt that, sir. There was much talk of gold, of course, and stories of discoveries in the Far West, but nothing came of it, nothing at all."

"Men did go out there, however?"

"A few. Adventurers or fools. Oh, yes! I believe the French government did send a military detachment to the West at one time, but that was very long ago."

"Did you know any of those who went west?"

"No . . . no, I think not. We were planting sugar then and were much too busy to think of such things. And I believe very few did go."

"What of Pierre?" his wife suggested.

"Pierre?" he frowned. "Oh, yes! But that was later. He never came back, so we never did know what he went after, exactly. Some wild-goose chase, I expect.

The Bastons were a mixed lot. Not very steady, you know. Chopping about from one thing to another. They still are, for that matter."

"Charles!"

"Well, it's true, and you know it. That Andre, for example, he is nothing but a—"

Suddenly a man was standing by the table. "You were saying, LaCroix?"

Orrin glanced up. The man was tall and broad, strongly built with a face that might have been carved from granite. The eyes were cold and blue, the face clean-shaven but for a waxed mustache.

"You were speaking of me, LaCroix?"

Orrin was shocked when he glanced at the old man, for his face had gone white and stiff. He was frightened, but even as Orrin looked, the man's pride asserted itself and he started to rise.

Instantly, Orrin was on his feet. "I am afraid you have the advantage of me, sir. We were talking of my old neighbors, Andy and Bert Masters. Do you know them, then?"

"Who?"

Andre Baston faced sharply around.

"If you know them," Orrin said, smiling, "you'll understand. Andy, he was a moonshiner. Came from Tennessee and settled down here in the bayous and took to makin' whiskey—by the way, what did you say your name was? Mine is Sackett. Orrin Sackett."

"I'm Andre Baston. I do not understand you, sir." Andre's tone was cold. "I understood this man to say—"

"Sure you did. The Masters were a no-good lot. I never did figure that was even their name. Even the 'shine they made wasn't much, but one thing I'll give ol' Andy. He had him a couple of the best coon-hounds—"

"I am afraid there is some mistake," Andre said coldly. He stared into Orrin's eyes. "You, sir, I do not like."

Orrin chuckled. "Now, isn't that a coincidence? I was just about to say the same thing. I don't like you, either, but while we're on the subject, what did happen to Pierre?"

Andre's face went pale with shock, then reddened. Before he could speak, Orrin said, "Not that I care, but folks ask questions when a man disappears. Especially a man like Pierre. He wasn't alone, was he? Man should never go into wild country alone. Of course, that always raises the question of what happened to those who were with him? Did any of them get back?"

Orrin thrust out his hand. "Nice talking to you, Mr. Baston, maybe we can sit down for a real confidential talk one of these times."

Abruptly, Orrin sat down, and Andre Baston walked away.

The old man was sunken in his chair, his face gray. His wife looked across at Orrin. "Thank you, oh, thank you! You saved his life, you know. They have never liked us, and Andre Baston is a duelist."

"He is?" Orrin glanced at Andre. He was seating himself at the adjoining table. "Was he with Pierre on that trip west?"

For a moment there was no reply, and then the woman spoke softly. "We must go now, monsieur. It is late and my husband is tired."

LaCroix got to his feet slowly. For a moment Orrin thought he was about to fall, but he stiffened his shoulders. Then he looked down at Orrin. "I am not sure. I believe he was."

Orrin got to his feet. "I have enjoyed the conversation. If I can be of any assistance—"

"Thank you."

He sat down again, watching them walk slowly away, two fine, proud people.

Suddenly, a voice spoke. "Mr. Sackett? I am Fanny Baston, and my uncle is very sorry for the way he acted. He believed it was his name he heard."

Orrin Sackett looked up into the eyes of one of the most beautiful girls he had ever seen. Quickly, he got to his feet. "It was a natural mistake," he said.

"We must make amends. We would not wish you to leave New Orleans thinking us inhospitable." She put her hand on his. "Mr. Sackett, would you come to dinner at our home? Thursday night?"

"Of course," he said. "I'd be glad to come."

When she seated herself at her own table, she looked at her brother and uncle. "There!" she said. "Now it is up to you! What did we come here for, anyway?"

CHAPTER II

We Sacketts been going down to New Orleans ever since there was a town yonder. This time I wasn't going to see the lights or dance the fandango, but to help Orrin work out a trail.

The trail along which we had to read sign was twenty years cold, and it was the trail of our own father.

Pa was what you'd call a wandering man, a mountain man in his later years, who understood the trapping of fur and how to get along with the red man.

He had been to the shining mountains a time or two, but the last time he never come home. That wasn't so unusual as to raise sweat on a man, for those were parlous times, and many a man went west and nobody saw anything of him after that but maybe his hair at some Indian's belt.

We boys knew the country ways, and we figured pa was thrown from his horse somewhere on the high plains, got caught without water, or run short of powder and lead with the Indians closing in. There was a sight of things could happen to a body in western lands, and betwixt us we'd come up against most of them. The trouble was with ma.

She was growing old now, and with the passing of years her memories turned more and more to pa, and to wondering what had become of him. She was fearful he might be stove up and helpless somewhere back in the hills, or maybe held hostage by some Indians. Of a night ma didn't sleep very well, and she'd set up in her old rocker and worry about pa.

Now pa was a knowing kind of a man. He could

make do with mighty little, and, given time, he could edge himself out of any kind of a fix. We boys figured that if pa was alive he'd come home, one way or t'other.

We were living in New Mexico now. Tyrel was trying to sell his holdings near Mora, figuring on moving west to the new town of Shalako. Orrin was busy with his law practice, but he said he could take some time, and I guess I was actually free to roam. Anyway, no woman, except ma, would worry for me.

"I'll go to New Orleans, Tell," Orrin told me, "and I'll check what records I can find. When you come along down I'll try to have a starting place."

The three of us set down with ma to talk over pa's last days at home to find some clue to just where he was going. The Rockies are a wide and wonderful bunch of mountains, but they aren't just one range. There are hundreds of them, so where in the high-up hills do you begin to hunt for a man?

Do you start hunting sign in the Black Hills or the Big Belts? The Absarokas, Sawatch, or Sangre de Cristos? Do you search the Greenhorns, the Big Horns, Wind Rivers, San Juans, La Platas, the Needles, Mogollons, Uintas, Crazy Mountains, or Salish? The Abajos, Henrys, Peloncillos, the Chiricahuas, or the Snake Range? Do you cross the Black Rock Desert or the Painted? Do you search down in Hell's Canyon? On the Green or the Popo Agie?

Where do you hunt for one man where armies might be lost?

New Orleans was a far piece from the fur-trapped streams where the beaver build, but it was there the trail should begin, for it was there pa headed when he rode away from the Cumberland Hills of Tennessee.

Cities made me uneasy. A body couldn't blaze a trail in a city, and folks weren't out and out what they seemed. Usually, they made it a point to show one face while hiding another.

Orrin was city-wise. He could read city-sign the way I'd track a mustang horse across a flat-rock mesa. Of course, Orrin was also a fair hand at tracking and nigh as good in a shoot-out as me or Tyrel. Orrin had started early to reading law, packing a copy of Blackstone in his saddlebags and reading whenever there was time. He was also an upstanding, handsome man, and when he started to talk even the rocks and trees had to listen. We Sacketts were English and Welsh mostly, but Orrin must have taken after the Welsh, who have the gift of speaking with a song in their words.

New Orleans wasn't no new place to me, like I said. We Sacketts, along with other hill folks from Kentucky or Tennessee, been floating rafts of logs downstream for a coon's age, but the places I knew best weren't likely to be on Orrin's callin' list. Come to think of it most of those places were joints where I'd gone to roust out our shanty boys to get them started home. Places like Billy Phillip's 101 Ranch, Lulu White's Mahogany Hall, the Five Dollar House, and the Frenchman's. Or maybe Murphy's Dance House on Gallatin Street.

You had to be a man with the bark on to even go into those places. I never paid 'em much mind, but when you went down-river with a shanty-boat crew you wound up in some mighty rough places. I usually had to lead the fight that got them out, and those fights aren't for the delicate. It was fist, skull, an' batter 'em down, and you stayed on your feet or you got tromped.

The Saint Charles Hotel was a mighty fine place, the like of which I'd not seen before. In my dusty black suit and boots I didn't shape up to the kind of folks they quartered there.

The clerk had his hair slicked down like he'd been licked to be swallered, and he looked at me like I was something a dog dragged up on the porch. "Yes?" he said.

"I am hunting Orrin Sackett," I said. "He's bedded down here."

The clerk took down a big register and checked the list. "Oh, yes! Mr. Sackett. But he is no longer with us. He's been gone—let's see—he left on the twentieth, sir. He's been gone two days."

Now that just didn't set right. Orrin had said positive that he would meet me at the Saint Charles today. So if he was gone, he'd be back.

"You sure? He was to meet me here."

"I am sorry, sir. Mr. Sackett checked out and left no forwarding address."

"He took his duffle, his bags, an' like that?"

"Of course, he—" This gent held up suddenly like he'd thought of something. "When I think of it, he did leave his saddle here and a rifle, I believe."

Now I was worried. No Sackett goes off anywhere without a saddle and a Winchester. It just didn't stand to reason Orrin would.

"I guess you better let me have a room," I said. "The same room he had if it's available."

He hesitated, evidently not sure if I could stand the traffic, but I took out my poke and shook him out a couple of double eagles. "You set that by," I said, "an' when she's et up, you give me a whistle.

"Whilst you're about it, send up a tailor. I got to order some Sunday-go-to-meetin' clothes."

That room was most elegant. Had a big flowered bowl and pitcher, and there was a bathroom right down the hall. I set my gear down and took a quick look around. The room had been cleaned so there'd be nothing of Orrin's left, but I knew Orrin real well and had an idea where to look.

Under a corner of the rug, pasted there neat as could be, were two gold pieces. That was a trait of Orrin's— it was getaway money in case he got robbed or whatever. Now I knew for sure something was wrong, wrong as all get-out. If he had reason to leave his saddle and rifle, Orrin would never leave without his getaway money.

Right then I set down and went to figuring. Gettin' yourself robbed, knocked on the head, or killed in New Orleans in these 1870s was about the easiest thing a body could do, but Orrin was no pilgrim. He'd been where the bear walks an' the buzzard roosts, and he was uncommon shrewd in the ways of men.

About then I pulled up and set my saddle. Orrin was knowing in the ways of men, but his record was no good when it come to reading sign on women. Tyrel or me, we were more suspicious, maybe because women hadn't paid us so much mind as they had Orrin. He had takin' ways, and kind of expected women to like him, which they usually did. More than that, he was a downright friendly man, and if Orrin was in trouble you can bet there was a woman somewhere around. Of course, you can say that of most men.

After the tailor had come to measure me for a couple of suits, I talked to the boy who showed him up to the room. "This here room," I said, "was occupied until a couple of days ago by a handsome big man with a nice smile. You recall him?"

"I do."

"Now, I am his brother, so you can talk free. Did he have him a woman around?"

"He did not. He was in his room very little. I remember him, suh. He was most thoughtful, suh."

"Did you see him with anyone else? I've got to find him." I put a silver dollar in his hand. "You ask around. Come to me as soon as you hear tell of him and I'll have another of those for you."

Disappearing is one of the least easy things to do if a body has any recognizable way of living. We all set patterns, and if we break them somebody is sure to notice, although it may be somebody we don't even know.

Orrin was a man easy to notice and easy to remember. He never made it a point to be nice to folks . . . he just was. It was him. He was polite to everyone, a man folks talked to mighty easy, a man with a pleasant way about him who would sooner avoid trouble than have it. He could put you off guard and turn a conversation from trouble into casual talk better than anybody I ever knew.

At the same time he was strong, as strong as me, I expect, and I never took hold of anything that it didn't move. He was a fine boxer, a better than average Cornish-style wrestler, and a dead shot with either hand. Peaceful man though he was, I never knew anybody to take more pleasure in a plain or fancy knockdown and drag-out brawl. In spite of his easy-going ways, if you shaped up to tear down his meathouse you'd bought yourself a packet of trouble.

So I just idled about, listening and talking to a few folks about my brother, but nobody recalled anything helpful. People around the Saint Charles remembered

him and so did a boy at the corner who sold news-
papers, a man down the street at a secondhand book
store, and a girl who served him coffee a couple of
times in a restaurant down the street a few blocks. An
old Negro who drove a carriage for hire told me about
him going there.

It was a small place under a wrought-iron balcony.
There was a table near a wide window looking out on
the street.

Now I'm a coffee-drinking man and always kind of
had an urge for the coffee they brew down Louisiana
way, so I took a table by the window and a right pretty
girl with dark hair and dark eyes brought me coffee.
Right off I asked about Orrin.

"Oh, yes! I remember him very well, but he has not
been in lately. Not for two or three days."

"Did he come here often?"

"He surely did. And he always sat right where you're
sitting. He said he liked to watch people walking along
the street."

"Was he always alone?"

"Yes—always. I never even saw him speak to anyone until the last time he was in. He spoke to a lady
who comes in sometimes."

"Young?"

"Oh, no. Mrs. LaCroix is—well, she's past sixty, I'd
say."

"Did they have coffee?"

"Oh, no. They just spoke. Well, she did talk to him
a little. She was thanking him for something. I—I didn't
listen, you know, but I couldn't help but hear. It was
something that happened in the dining room at the Saint
Charles. I have no idea what it was about except that
Mr. Sackett avoided trouble for them, somehow."

Well, that was something.

Orrin never was much inclined to just sit around and
drink coffee, so if he came here more than once he had
him a reason. Orrin liked to watch the people pass, did
he?

What people? There was a lot of folks yonder, and
somebody was passin' every minute, but I had an idea
he wouldn't sit here just on the chance somebody

would pass . . . he must have known somebody would
go by there, or maybe there was somebody he could
watch from where he sat.

I sat there about half an hour when the waitress returned to my table. The other folks who had been drinking coffee were gone.

"Sit down," I suggested. "My front name is Tell,
short for William Tell, a man my pa favored for his
arrow shooting and his way of thinking. It's mighty nice,
just to set and watch the folks go by. I've seen more
people in the last half hour than I see in two months
out yonder where I've been, and I've never seen so
many people afoot."

She was amused. "Do you ride everywhere?"

"A man wouldn't be caught dead without a horse,
ma'am. Why, when Eb Farley was to be buried out
yonder they laid him out in the hearse nice an' proper,
an' d'you know what the corpse done? He got right up
out of the coffin, straddled a horse, an' rode all the way
to the bone yard; then he crawled back into the coffin
and they buried him peaceful."

At that moment a man walked out of the saloon
across the street. He was a huge man with heavy shoulders, the biggest hands and feet I ever did see, and a
wide, flat face. He wore boots, a red sash about his
waist, and a nondescript gray coat and pants.

"Who's *that?*"

She looked quickly, then away. "Don't let him see
you looking at him. That's Hippo Swan. He's a notorious bully. He used to be overseer at the Baston planta-
tion before they lost their slaves. Now he just hangs
around the dance-saloons."

When I returned to the hotel I went to the desk. "Did
my brother leave no message at all when he left?" I
asked.

"As a matter of fact, Mr. Sackett, I did not see your
brother that day. He sent a messenger for his valise."

"Just that? No written message?"

"Of course. We would never give a guest's bag-
gage to anyone without an order. In fact, we have it
on file." He got out the message. It was written on

ordinary tablet paper, and the handwriting was nothing like my brother's excellent script.

Opening the register to my brother's entry I laid the two signatures side by side. There was no resemblance.

The clerk's face grew flushed. "I am sorry, sir. I think I had better call the manager."

CHAPTER III

Up in my room, I sat down to do some figuring. Orrin was surely in trouble, and it was serious trouble by the look of it. He was not a man to seek difficulties, and he had a smooth tongue for them when they came, so what could have happened?

He had not returned to his room. Somebody else had picked up his luggage, using a forged note to do it. Whoever came for the valise hadn't dreamed there'd be a rifle and saddle locked up at the hotel. Folks visiting in New Orleans rarely came equipped like that,

Looked to me like the only lead I had was that woman he'd spoken to in the coffee shop—Mrs. LaCroix—the name was not uncommon.

She had been in the dining room of the Saint Charles, and Orrin had helped her with some difficulty. Now that would be like Orrin. No Sackett ever stood by with a woman needing help. Looked to me like the dining room was the place to start inquiries.

Missing two days . . . I was scared.

Orrin could be just one of many to be robbed or killed. The only lead I had was what took place in the dining room and that might be nothing at all. Of course, there was that time, years back, when we came down-river with a raft of logs and had that shindig on the river front, but more than likely nobody remembered that. Still, a look along the dance-saloon route might turn up something.

Come to think of it, I had a friend down yonder. There was a woman down there, a mighty notorious woman now, from what I heard. She'd been a hard case even as a youngster when I helped her out a couple of times. Brick-top Jackson was now figured to be as tough as they come, a mighty handsome woman with a figure like nothing you ever saw, but a woman who could, and would, fight like the dirtiest waterfront brawler you ever did see. Brick-top was a thief, a murderer, and a lot of other things, but she would know what was happening along the mean streets, and maybe she would tell me.

There was a tap on the door. I took up my Colt and shoved it down behind my waistband, then opened the door.

It was that Negro bell man that I'd given the dollar to.

"Mr. Sackett?" He stepped in and closed the door behind him. "I have some information, suh."

Well, I went down into my pocket for a dollar, but he wasn't hungry. He said, "Your brother had an altercation, suh. He exchanged a few words with Mr. Baston, suh."

"Baston?" Where had I heard that name?

"Andre Baston, suh."

He said it like it was a name I should know. When I looked puzzled he said, "Andre Baston is thought by some to be the most dangerous man in New Orleans, suh. He has killed twelve men . . . in duels, suh; with pistol, knife, or rapier he is considered the best."

In some places that might not have meant so much, but New Orleans was no ordinary town.

"What happened?"

Briefly, he explained what had happened in the dining room, but it did not come to much. There had been some words, but it was purely a small matter, and, had anybody but this here Baston been involved, nobody would have paid it much mind.

"Those people he was talking to? Was their name La-Croix?"

"Yes, suh. It was. They are fine people, very fine people, suh."

"And the Bastons?"

This Negro was a fine-looking man of fifty or so, with an inborn dignity and obviously some education. His distaste for gossip was evident, but there was something more here, too. Now I ain't given to second sight, but feelings show through, and it was right plain that this man liked the LaCroix people, but not the Bastons.

"There are many Bastons, suh. Some of them fine people. Most of them, in fact. Old Mr. Philip, suh . . . before the war, suh, I was one of his people. He was a fine man, a fine man."

"What about Andre?"

He hesitated. "Mr. Sackett, I would have no dealings with him, suh."

"You did say he had killed twelve men."

"I said he had killed twelve men in duels, suh. There have been others, suh, when the arrangements were less formal."

Well, that didn't get me anywhere. Orrin had exchanged a few words with Baston and they had parted. If I could talk to the LaCroix people they could tell me what was said, but the lead did not look promising. It looked to me like Orrin had just dropped off the world.

Two days more of hunting and inquiring left me exactly where I was when I arrived. Now Orrin had been missing four days. And then I located the LaCroix family.

When I was shown into the library where they were sitting they seemed surprised. Mr. LaCroix got up quickly, but he was a mite stiff, I could see. He was a fine-looking man, well up in years. "Mr. Sackett? I am sorry. I was expecting—"

"My brother, I guess. Orrin's a sight better looking than me."

"You are—"

"William Tell Sackett, ma'am. Fact is, I came to see if you had seen my brother?"

"Seen him? Of course. He sat beside us at dinner one night, and I believe Mrs. LaCroix saw him at the coffee shop one day."

"Yes, I did. It was a chance meeting but a fortunate one as I wished to thank him again."

"Sir? What happened that night? I mean, if you don't mind. You see, Orrin's been missing for four days."

Well, they exchanged a look, and it was a scared look.

"If you could tell me just what happened, it might help," I suggested. "I've heard a good deal as far as Baston is concerned, but what happened there in the dining room?"

Betwixt them, they laid it out for me, and all of it made sense except that last question about what happened to Pierre. When I brought that up they told me Orrin said he was interested in some mining claims out in the San Juans, which is about what Orrin would say to cover his reasons for asking questions. It might give him a lead on somebody who left New Orleans for the wild lands to the west, as it seemed likely to have done.

It began to look like Orrin had thrown that Pierre question in there on chance. It was one of his lawyer's tricks, and it had taken Andre Baston off guard . . . but it might have gotten Orrin killed, too. A body just didn't play games with a man like Baston.

"This Andre Baston now? Was he alone?"

"He was joining his niece, Fanny, and nephew at a table near your brother.

"And this Pierre they spoke of?"

"Pierre Bontemps. He was Andre's brother-in-law. He went west on some wild venture. Pierre was that way, always going off somewhere at the least excuse. He was killed out there, by Indians, it was said. Andre got back."

It still didn't shape up to much. Orrin had exchanged a few words with a man with a reputation as a duelist, and he had said something to which I gathered Baston's reaction was mighty strong.

A few more questions, and it began to look like when pa went west it was with Pierre Bontemps, Andre Baston, and some others. I had no idea how many others and who they were.

After a little more talk I got into a carriage and returned to the Saint Charles. When I stepped down from the carriage, Hippo Swan was standing on the curb opposite the hotel. And when I saw him I remembered where I'd heard the name Baston before. The girl in the coffee shop had said he had once worked for someone named Baston.

When I reached the door, I glanced back. Hippo Swan was lighting a cigar, but he was holding the match up higher than necessary, or so it seemed to me.

A signal? If so, to whom?

Well, now. Chances were I was just seeing shadows where none existed, but it costs nothing to play it safe. Nobody had left any messages at the desk for me so I started on up to my room.

The window, I recalled, looked over the street out front. A body standing in that window could easily see a match struck down there on the street.

Turning around on the stairs I went back down to the desk. The clerk was gone, but the Negro I'd talked to earlier was standing there.

"Is there anyone in the room adjoining mine? The one with the door opening into mine?"

He consulted the register. "Not at present, suh."

I put a silver dollar on the desk. "Could you let me have it for a few minutes?"

He looked straight into my eyes. "What seems to be the trouble, Mr. Sackett?"

"Well, now. I'm kind of a cautious man. It seems to me that one Sackett disappearing is enough, and if somebody was inside my room now, somebody who was waiting for me, he'd be likely to be waiting beside the hall door."

"It is likely, suh." He pushed the key toward me and my dollar as well. "Would you like me to call the hotel officer, suh?"

"Thank you . . . no."

Turning away I started for the steps. He spoke after me. "Good hunting, suh."

I walked softly down the carpeted hall and opened the room next to mine, then ever so gently I put the key into the lock, careful to make no sound. I ran quickly around to my own door, fumbled with the knob, then swore softly, muttering something about the key.

I ran back to the door in the adjoining room and opened it suddenly.

There was a little light from the window, and the

bulk of a man waiting by the door. A shadow moved as the door swung wide . . . there was *another man!*

They came for me, both of them. They were big men and were probably considered quite tough. They came for me, one from each direction. I had my knife and I had my Colt, but the Colt seemed an unfair advantage, and no doubt there was folks asleep upstairs or around me. I stepped in to meet them as they came at me from two sides, but I hooked a toe behind a chair and kicked it in front of the one coming from the right, and, as he fell over it, I lowered the boom on the second one with a good right fist.

He was ambitious, that gent was, and he was coming in fast, so when he met my right fist halfway he was driving right into it with all the thrust of his legs.

There was a *splat,* then a crunch, as his nose folded like an accordion under my fist. As he hit the floor I kicked him in the side of the head.

The first man was starting to get up, but I was through fooling around. I put the point of my knife against his throat right over the jugular vein, and I said, "I don't care if I do or I don't. What d' you think?"

He was sure of one thing, and he didn't need to be sure of anything else. One twist of that blade and to-morrow morning they'd be throwing dirt over him.

He held right still. "For God's sake, mister! Don't kill me! I didn't mean nothin'!"

"Who set you up to this?"

"I don't—"

That knife point dug a mite deeper. A tiny push now and he'd be bleeding on the carpet. "You tell me. You tell me who sent you and what you were to do with me."

"Swan sent me. The Hippo. We was to lay you out and pack you out the back way and down to the swamp."

"Get up, then." I took a step back and let him up, and I didn't much care if he wanted to open the ball or not, but he'd had all he wanted. There was a trickle of blood down his neck and it scared him. He was only scratched, but he didn't know how much and he was so scared he was ready to cry.

"Take that," I pointed my foot at the other man, "and clear out of here. Next time you tackle a Sackett, you be sure his hands are tied."

He backed away from me. "I had nothin' to do with that. It was him," he gestured to the man on the floor, "an' Hippo. They done it."

For a moment I looked at him, then, the edge of my blade up, I stepped toward him. "Where did they take him?"

His voice was a whisper. "To the swamp. To a houseboat on the bayou. I don't know which one."

"Get out!"

He stooped, lifting the other man with an effort, and staggered out. Closing the door after him I lit the light, then I closed and locked the door to the adjoining room. There was a spot of blood on the point of my knife and I wiped it clean.

There was a light tap on the door. It was the Negro again. "The key, suh? I supposed you might be through with it."

"Thanks—I am. But I believe I've broken a chair."

He glanced at it. "I hope that wasn't all," he said quietly. He gathered the pieces. "A chair can be replaced."

"What's your name?" I asked him, suddenly aware that I wanted to know.

He did not smile. "Judas, suh. Judas Priest."

Thank you, Judas."

The Negro turned at the door. "Two of them, suh? That's doing very well, suh."

"You saw them?"

"Oh, yes, suh! Of course." He slipped his hand into his pocket, and it came out wearing a very formidable set of brass knuckles. "We couldn't allow anything to happen to a guest! Not at the Saint Charles, suh!"

"Much obliged. That's what I'd call service. I'd better put in a good word for you to the management."

"If you don't mind, suh, my participation would have been entirely my own responsibility."

"Thank you, Judas."

He drew the door shut after him, and I dropped down on the bed. Orrin was in a houseboat on a bayou. That was mighty little to know, for there were dozens of bayous and probably hundreds of houseboats.

Orrin might be dead, or dying. Right now he might be needing all the help he could get.

And I could not help him . . .

CHAPTER IV

Settin' on the side of the bed I gave thought to my problem. I had to find Orrin and almighty quick. They had no reason I could think of for keepin' him alive, but Orrin was a glib-tongued man and if anybody could find them a reason, he could.

There seemed no rhyme or reason to it. Most killings these days started from nothing, some measly argument that suddenly becomes all-fired important. But even allowing for that there still seemed to be more to it.

When it came right down to it, I had little to go on, and nobody ever accused me of being brighter than average. I can handle any kind of a fightin' weapon as good or better than most, and I'm rawhide tough and bull-strong, but when it comes to connivin' I ain't up to it. Straight out an' straight forward, that's me.

Orrin had come to town lookin' for some sign of that Frenchman who had gone off with pa to the western mountains, and a small chance of finding it, yet somehow he had evidently come up with something. Then, settin' at table he had struck up conversation with those LaCroix people and a name had been dropped. Out of the words that followed, Orrin, always good at keeping a witness off balance, asked what had become of Pierre? And he struck a nerve.

Pierre had not returned from a trip to the western lands. Andre Baston had been on that trip. Andre had not liked that question about Pierre, so what could a body figure from that? Maybe he had run out and left Pierre in a fight. Maybe he had taken something that belonged to Pierre . . . and maybe he had killed Pierre.

All that was speculation, and a man can get carried

away by a reasonable theory. Often a man finds a theory that explains things and he builds atop that theory, finding all the right answers . . . only the basic theory is wrong. But that's the last thing he will want to admit.

Pa had left New Orleans for the western lands at about that time. The name Sackett had jolted Andre when Orrin spoke it. And right after Orrin had introduced himself as a Sackett and prodded Andre Baston with the name of Pierre, Orrin disappeared.

What I had to do now was find one houseboat where there might be four or five hundred, and the only way I knew to look was to head for Gallatin Street, and after that the swamp. I spoke reasonable Spanish of a Mexican sort, and a few odd words of French, picked up in Louisiana or up along the Canadian border. I'd need them words. New Orleans had been a French and Spanish city for nearly a hundred years before it became American, and a lot of folks along the bayous spoke only French, like along the Bayou Teche, where the Cajuns lived.

First off, I needed somebody who knew the bayous, so I'd start down yonder where folks have all manner of secret knowledge. Time was I knowed a few folks. Somebody had told me Brick-top was gone.

Brick-top Jackson was meaner than a grizzly bear with a sore tooth and apt to be on the prod most of the time. There toward the end she hung out with a man named Miller who had an iron ball where his hand had been. One time he come home with a whip and tried to take it to her. She took the whip from him and beat him half to death, so he tried a knife, and she took that and fed it to him five or six times. Miller got tired of it then and up and died on her. They'd fit many a time before, but he spited her this time, and when the law came and found him they carted the Brick-top off to prison.

At one time I'd helped her a mite, not even knowing who she was, and I don't know whether that surprised her more than me going on about my business. Only she told folks I was one man she'd go to hell for. I think she went to hell for a lot of men.

But along the river a man meets a sight of strange

people, and I never had no preaching in mind. I'd made a friend hither and yon, and it seemed likely there were a few down on the mean streets, so I went there.

The folks who decided what sin was never walked Gallatin Street in its wild days. Had they done so, their catalogue of evil would have stretched out a good bit, and we'd have a hundred commandments rather than ten. It was thieving, brawling, and murderous. There was the Blue Anchor, the Baltimore, the Amsterdam, and Mother Burke's Den. (The Canton House was closed after Canton kicked a sailor to death.) Nobody needed to hunt for a place in which to get drunk or robbed, and nine times out of ten if it was one it was surely the other.

Tarantula juice was the cheapest drink, two gallons of raw alcohol, a shaved plug of tobacco and half a dozen burnt peaches mixed in a five-gallon keg of water. If they stinted on anything it was the alcohol, but in the meaner dives they were inclined to add almost anything to make up the volume.

From joint to joint I went, keeping a weather eye open for a face I knew. All were familiar. I guess you could find them on any waterfront in the world, swaggering, tough, ready with fist or knife, and in Murphy's dance-saloon I struck it rich. I'd ordered a beer—his beer was usually safe—and was looking around when a tall, slim man with a gold ring in his ear came up alongside me.

He was a long-jawed man with yellow eyes, and he was wearing a planter's hat with a bandana tied beneath it and a brown coat with a scarf about his neck. He was thin, but with a whipcord look of strength about him.

"You can trust the beer, Sackett, and Murphy too, up to a point."

"Thanks," I said, "but can I trust a stranger with a ring in his ear?"

"I'm the Tinker," he said, and that explained everything to a man from our hills.

The Tinker was a tinker, he was also a pack-peddler who roamed the back mountain trails to sell or trade whatever he could. He was a man from foreign places who seemed always to have been amongst us, and although he looked thirty he might have been ninety. He had wandered the lonely roads through the Cumberlands and the Smokies and the Blue Ridge. They knew him on the Highland Rim, and from the breaks of the Sandy to the Choccoloco. Among other things, he made knives of a kind like you've never seen, knives sold to few, given to none.

"I'm glad to see you, then, for I need someone who knows the bayous."

"I know them a little," he said, "and I know those who know them better. I have people here."

The Tinker was a gypsy, and among that society he was held in vast respect. Whether he was a king among them, or a worker of magic, or simply a better man with steel, I never knew.

"They've got Orrin," I said. "A man named Andre Baston's behind it, and Hippo Swan."

"When a Sackett breeds enemies," the Tinker said, "he never looks among the weak for them. They are a wicked lot, Tell Sackett."

"You know me then?"

"I was among them who rode to the Mogollon when trouble was upon you there. I rode with your cousin Lando, who is my friend. Where will you be if I have anything to tell you?"

"The Saint Charles. If I am not in, there is a man of color there, Judas Priest, you may speak to him."

"I know the man, and who does not?"

"You know him, too?"

"He is a friend to have."

The Tinker stood away from the bar and motioned to a man who loafed not far away. He put his hand on my arm. "This is Tell Sackett, a friend of mine."

"Of course," he said.

The Tinker looked around at me. "Now you will not be bothered," he said. "Go where you will in New Orleans but I cannot answer for the swamp or the bayous."

All around us was a sweaty, pushing, swearing, pocket-picking, poke-slitting lot, but now as I turned to leave they rolled away from me, and the way was easy. Among the crowd I saw the Tinker's friend and some others with him, and usually one of them was close to me.

The gypsies had their own way of doing things in New Orleans, and there were always more of them about than one believed.

I was tired from my search through the dives. I turned back toward the hotel when suddenly Hippo Swan was before me. "Bring him to the Saint Charles, Hippo," I said. "If I have to come after him, you will deal with me."

He laughed, and glanced around for his men, but they had disappeared and there was an open space around us. He did not like it. He was afraid of no man, but something had happened here that he could not judge, for he had come with a half dozen men and now he was alone.

He had white skin, thick lips, and small, cruel eyes almost hidden under thick flesh. He was even larger than I had at first believed, with great, heavy shoulders and arms, and hands both broad and thick.

"I will deal with you, will I? I shall like that, me bucko, oh, I shall like that!" he said.

I did not like the man. There is that in me that bristles at the bully, and this man was such a one. Yet he was not to be taken lightly. This man was cruel because he liked being cruel.

"If he's harmed, Hippo, I'll let the fish have what's left of you."

He laughed again. Oh, he was not worried by me. I always thought a threat an empty thing, but in this case I had a brother to help, and if a threat might hold them off even a little, I'd use it.

"What's one Sackett more or less?" he scoffed.

"Nothing to you, but a lot to the rest of us."

"Us? I see only one."

I smiled at him. "Hippo," I said quietly, "there are as many of us as there need to be. I've never seen more than a dozen at one time except when great-grandpa and great-grandma had their wedding anniversary. There were more than a hundred men. I did not count them all."

He didn't believe me. Neither did he like the way his

men disappeared from around him, nor the look of some of the dark, strange faces in the crowd. Perhaps they were the same he had always seen, but suddenly they must have seemed different.

"I'll choose my time," he muttered, "and I'll break you—like *that!*" He made a snapping motion with hands that looked big enough to break anything, and then he walked away from me, and I went back to the Saint Charles and changed my clothes for dinner.

My new suit had come, and it fit exceedingly well. All the clothes I'd had since the time ma wove and stitched them with her own hands I'd either made myself from buckskin or they were hand-me-downs from the shelves of cattle-town stores.

It seemed to me that I looked very fine, and I looked away from the mirror, suddenly embarrassed. After all, why get big ideas? I was nothing but a country boy, a hill boy if you wish, who'd put in a few years and a few calluses on his hands from work and on his behind from saddles.

What was I doing here in this fine suit? How many times would I wear it? And what was I doing in this fine hotel? I was a man of campfires, line camps, and bunkhouses, a drifter with a rope and a saddle and very little else. And I'd better never forget it.

Yet sometimes things can make a man forget. Orrin had a right to trust women. He was easy to look at, and he had a foot for the dancing and an ear for the music and a voice to charm the beaver out of their ponds.

None of that was true of me. I was a big, homely man—with wide shoulders, big hands, and a face like a wedge: hard cheekbones, and a few scars picked up from places where I shouldn't have been, maybe. I had scars on my heart, too, from the few times I'd won, only to lose again.

Soft carpets and white linen and the gleam of expensive glass and silver, they weren't for the likes of me. I was a man born to the smell of pine knots burning, to sleeping under the stars or under a chuck wagon, maybe, or to the smell of branding fires or powder-smoke.

Yet I polished my boots some, and slicked back my

hair as best I could, and, with a twist at my mustache, I went down the stairs to the dining room.

The traps that life lays for a man are not always of steel, nor is the bait what he'd expect.

When I came through the door she was setting there alone, and when she looked up at me her eyes seemed to widen and a sort of half-smile trembled on her lips.

She was beautiful, so beautiful I felt my heart ache with the sight of her. Suddenly scared, I made a start to turn away, but she got to her feet quickly but gracefully, and she said, "Mr. Sackett? William Tell Sackett?"

"Yes, ma'am." I twisted my hat in my hands. "Yes, ma'am. I was just aimin' to set for supper. Have you had yours yet?"

"I was waiting for you," she said, and dropped her eyes. "I am afraid you'll think me very bold, but I . . ."

"No such thing," I said. I drew back a chair for her. "I surely dread eatin' supper alone. Seems to me I'm the only one alone, most of the time."

"Have you been alone a lot, Mr. Sackett?"

She looked up at me out of those big, soft eyes and I couldn't swallow. Not hardly.

"Yes, ma'am. I've traveled wild country a sight, and away out in the mountains and upon the far plains a body sets alone . . . although there's camp-robber jays or sometimes coyotes around."

"You must be awfully brave."

"No, ma'am. I just don't know no better. It comes natural when you've growed—grown—up with it."

My collar felt tight, but then I never did like them stiff collars. They chafed my neck. My gun had twisted over on my belly and was gouging me. I could feel the sweat on my forehead and I desperately wanted to wipe it away.

"Your face looks so—so hard! I mean the skin! Like mahogany."

"It ain't much," I said, "although it cuts less than most. Why, I mind the time—"

Well, I caught myself in time. That there was no story for a genteel girl like this here. She suddenly put her hand up to my face.

"Do you mind? I just have to see if it's as hard as it

looks!" Her hand was soft, like the feathers on a dove. I could feel my heart pounding, and I was afraid she'd hear it. It had been a long time since any woman made up to me like that.

Suddenly somebody was beside the table. "Mr. Sackett, suh? A message for you, suh." And then in a slightly different tone, he said, and it was Judas talkin', "How do you do, Miss Baston?"

CHAPTER V

That name did just what Judas figured it would do and brought me right down out of the clouds. He shot down my balloon with one word, and it was well he did so, because it was only filled with hot air, anyway. No girl like this one would set her cap for a man like me unless there was double-dealing in it.

She smiled just as brightly, but it seemed to me there was a mean kind of anger in her eyes. Right then she could have shot Judas Priest.

For a moment there I forgot the message I had in my hand, but it was Fanny Baston who brought my attention back to it.

Judas had disappeared without even getting a reply from her, but I reckon he wasn't expecting one. Miss Baston glanced at the note in my hand. "Something always interrupts whenever I start talkin' to a good-looking man, Mr. Sackett. You can attend to that later, if you don't mind."

I just smiled at her. I had my good sense back now, or part of it. "It might be important."

Unfolding the note, I read: *Absinthe House. 11 o'clock tonight.* And it was signed with a profile of the Tinker. One quick, but amazingly lifelike line.

I folded the note and put it in my shirt pocket and buttoned down the flap. I had a feeling she was itching to put her dainty white hands on it. She'd get it only over my dead body. I had a feeling she'd thought of that, too.

"I was lookin' forward to meetin' you, ma'am," I said, and then I lied to her. "Orrin, he said he'd met you and was plannin' to see you soon."

Her eyelids flickered with annoyance. She had not expected that, but folks who deal in crime should recall that folks like to talk, and will tell most everything, given a chance. She had no way of knowing that I hadn't seen or heard from Orrin.

"I am afraid you have gathered the wrong impression," she said. "I only met your brother briefly, but I found him most attractive. As a matter of fact, that was why I came here tonight. He was to have called on us and did not, and then they told me you were here. Where is your brother?"

"I was just goin' to ask you that question, ma'am. He's a man never fails to keep an appointment, so something serious must have happened. We had some business here in town."

"If we could help, Mr. Sackett, you have only to ask. We have many friends here. Our people have lived in New Orleans since shortly after it was founded."

"Must have been mighty hard on the menfolks back in those times," I said. "There weren't many women around. Not until they sent in the correction girls."

Bienville, when he was governor down here and had girls sent in from France to make wives for his men, got a shipload of eighty-eight or nine girls from a prison or "house of correction" in Paris. They were a bad lot, causing no end of trouble, so after that they shipped in some girls from the better classes, each of which was given a small chest of clothing and what not. These were a good lot of girls, serious and skilled at making a home, and they were called *filles à la cassette*—the casket girls.

Now as New Orleans folks have told me, nobody wanted to claim a correction girl as an ancestor, so the way it sounds all those girls died without issue, as the saying goes. And everybody who claims ancestry from those days claims a casket girl. This I knew from talk I'd heard, but I played it like I never heard of casket girls.

"No reason why some of those correction girls

shouldn't have turned out all right," I said. "You've no reason to be shamed by it."

Her face flushed angrily and she said sharply, "We had nothing to do with correction girls, Mr. Sackett! The Bastons descended from a very fine family—"

"I've no doubt," I agreed. "Anyway, a mill doesn't turn on water that's past, and no doubt your folks are contributing a great deal to the welfare of Louisiana right now. Why, I'd say there's probably a number of upstanding citizens among them."

From all I'd heard I knew the family had pretty much gone to seed. Philip was the only one folks seemed to respect. The others had pride, an old home, and a willingness to do anything as long as it wasn't work. One branch of the family had turned out honorable men, planters, public servants, soldiers, and the like; the other, and that was the line Andre and Fanny belonged to, had turned to gambling, spending, slave trading in the days when they could, and a lot of questionable activities.

Fanny Baston did not like me. I could see that plain, and she was very rapidly beginning to wish she'd never come here on what was, I suspected, a kind of fishing expedition.

Yet she stuck to the job, I'll give her that. "If you have business we would be glad to help. Would you mind telling me what it is?"

Now I'd been giving thought to all of this, and it seemed to me there could be only two reasons for the Bastons getting all heated up. They were afraid we were trying to discover something or uncover something.

They'd likely not be interested unless there was money in it. Pa had taken off to the western mountains with Pierre . . . for what?

It looked to me like Pierre knew, or thought he knew, where there was gold. From the fact that the trip was supposed to be a quick one, the gold must have been dug already, which meant hidden treasure.

"As a matter of fact," I said, "Orrin an' me were trying to trace down our pa. He disappeared down this-away some years back."

"Isn't it possible that he's dead?"

"Surely is, ma'am, only we want to *know*. Ma's getting on in years, and she worries about it. I suspect pa went west guiding some hunters, if he didn't get himself killed right here in town. Anyway, soon's we find out we're going home."

"To Tennessee?"

"No, ma'am. We live in New Mexico now, but we're fixing to move to Colorado and settle in the La Plata mountain country. Some of the boys are already there. Tyrel's in Santa Fe . . . unless he's on his way down here."

"Here?" Seemed to me there was anxiety in her voice, and I guess she was wondering how many she'd have to deal with.

"Yes, ma'am. Tyrel may come, too. He's the best of the lot at uncovering things. He's been a marshal in several towns out yonder. He's used to investigations."

We ordered some grub and talked of this and that for a while. It was early yet, and I had time to waste until that meeting with the Tinker. If he'd sent for me it meant he'd uncovered something, and it had to be something pretty positive or he wouldn't call me.

Fanny seemed anxious to leave Orrin out of it, and she chatted away, telling stories about the French Quarter, the old homes, and the plantations. "I'd love to show you ours," she told me. "It is a lovely old place, magnificent oaks with long Spanish moss trailing from them, flowers, green lawns . . . it is lovely!"

"I'll bet it is," I said, and meant it. There were some beautiful places around, and as for me, if I had to be in a city, there was no place I'd rather be in than New Orleans . . . if I had time on my hands. It had beauty and it had atmosphere, and as for the mean streets, well, they added color and excitement to the town.

"You mentioned Colorado," Fanny said. "Where do you plan to live?"

"Like I said, some of the boys have settled on the La Plata. That's pretty much down in the southwestern corner, just beyond the San Juans."

Well, I'm too old a fisherman not to know when I'd had a nibble, and I had one. Just what it was about her expression I don't know, but I knew she was interested when I mentioned the San Juans.

Now that's no little string of hills. There are fourteen peaks that go up fourteen thousand feet or more, and that's some of the most rugged country in the world. When it starts to snow back in there you either light a shuck and get out fast or you dig in for the winter.

"What is it like? I have never seen a mountain."

Well, I just looked at her, but I wasn't seeing her. I was seeing the La Plata River where it comes down from the mountain country, picking up little streams as it comes along, tumbling over the rocks, shaded by trees, chilled by the snow water, catching the color of the sky and the shadows of clouds. The stillness of beaver ponds, broken only by the widening V of a beaver swimming, mirroring the trunks of the aspen, catching the gold of the sun. Canyons quiet as the day after the earth was born, heights where the air was so clear the miles vanished and the faraway mountains of New Mexico showed themselves through the purple haze.

"Ma'am," I said, "I don't know what it is you are wishful for in this life, but you set down of a night and you pray to God that he'll let you walk alone across a mountain meadow when the wild flowers are blooming.

"You pray he'll let you set by a mountain stream with sunlight falling through the aspens, or that he'll let you ride across an above-timberline plateau with the strong bare peaks around you and the black thunderheads gathering around them—great, swelling rain clouds ready to turn the meadows into swamp in a minute or two . . . you let him show you those things, ma'am, and you'll never miss heaven if you don't make it.

"There's majesty in those peaks, ma'am, and grandeur in the clouds, and there's a far and wonderful beauty in the distance.

"Have you never looked upon distance, ma'am? Have you never pulled up your horse where your trail drops off into a black, deep canyon? Brimful with darkness and shadow? Or seen a deer pause on the edge of a meadow and lift its head to look at you? Standing there still as the trees around you to watch it? Have you never seen the trout leaping in a still mountain lake? Ma'am, I have, and before God . . . that's *country!*"

For a moment she sat still, looking at me. "You are a strange man, Tell Sackett, and I don't believe I should know you long."

She got up suddenly. "You would ruin me for what I want, and I'd ruin you because of what I am."

"No, ma'am, I would not ruin you for what you want because all those things you want don't amount to anything. They are just little bits of fluff and window dressing that you think will make you look better in the eyes of folks.

"You think maybe having a mite more money will build a wall around you to keep you from what's creeping up on you, but it won't. Out there where I come from, there's folks that want the same things you do and will go just as far to get them, but all of them wind up on the short end of the stick.

"As for me, ma'am, I wouldn't ruin as easy as you might think. There's nothing you could offer me that I'd swap for one afternoon ride through the hills, and I mean it. Once a man has lived with mountains you can't offer him a home with a prairie dog."

She walked away from me then and I stood and watched her go, a beautiful woman, beautifully gowned. Never did I see a woman walk away from me but I regretted it. I had no woman now. Ange was gone. We'd had something fine there, for a little while. As for Dorset—she'd gone off and I did not know if ever we'd meet again.

Sitting alone, I had another glass of wine and thought about what was to come.

I knew the Absinthe House. It was a popular place in New Orleans, and a lot of the young bloods did their drinking there, and their meeting of each other. It was on a busy corner where two people meeting would not be noticed much.

I paid my bill and went out into the quiet warmth of the street. There were many people there, strolling, talking, laughing. From the cafés and the dance-saloons there was music, but I walked down along the avenue, hearing little of the talk, pausing from time to time to check my back trail.

At the corner where the Absinthe House stood there were many people walking back and forth. I went into the café, glanced around at the crowd there and saw no familiar face. As I turned, a short, thickset man appeared close to my side. "This way, m'sieu." When we stepped around the corner, the Tinker was standing by a covered carriage.

We got in, the thickset man climbed to the driver's seat, and we rolled away.

"We have found him, I think. And there will be trouble."

"All right," I replied, "just let's get to him in time."

We turned into darker and darker streets. I recognized a sign here and there, and then at last we drew to a stop I heard somebody singing from a shack close by, a lonely, sad-sounding song.

Leaving our cab we started down a dark alleyway. A cat sprang away from beneath our feet. Somebody threw a bottle from a window and it broke upon other bottles. We went up a few wooden steps to a small dock by the river.

All was still. No lights shone from this dock. From the neighboring dock, an open window cast a gleam of light upon the dark, swirling waters of the river.

A boat was tied there, bumping against the underpinning of the dock, and on the shore a man waited. A dark man in a striped shirt that fit tightly over powerful muscles.

By the sound of his French he was a Cajun. He led the way down to the boat, and then we pushed off. There were three other men in the boat. I balanced myself on a thwart amidships and watched them hoist the small brown sail. There was little wind, but we caught what there was and moved out on the dark water.

We were off to find Orrin. Please God, he'd be alive.

"Quietly," the Tinker said, "it must be done quietly. They have more friends close by than we."

"You have a blade?" The man in the striped shirt asked.

"I do," I said, and no further words were spoken as we moved out along the river.

The night was still and warm. My mouth felt dry, and I was uneasy in the boat. I was at home in a saddle, but not here. My hand went again to the knife.

CHAPTER VI

The wind died, lost in the surrounding trees and brush. The only sound was the chunk of the oar at the stern. The water shone a dull black. Overhead a few stars showed themselves faintly in the ribbon of sky the trees permitted us to see.

We passed several boats tied up along shore, all dark and still. Twice we passed cabins where lights still showed, and from one came drunken arguing and shouting. We moved on, ghostlike, along the bayou.

I wondered if Orrin would be alive. There was small chance of it, although the Tinker, who had access to much information, believed he was.

I shucked my coat, wishing I had left it behind, but there had been nowhere to leave it. A man did not appear coatless in the evening at the Saint Charles.

"Not much further," someone said, and I touched the haft of my knife.

Orrin lay bound in the darkness. Now and then a spider or a daddy longlegs crept over his face. His shirt was soaked with perspiration, even where it had been stiff with blood. He needed a drink desperately, but the men who held him prisoner could not care less about his comfort.

They believed he knew something, believed he was after gold. Not for one minute had they bought the idea that he was only looking for information about his father. Somehow, something he had said had blown the lid off. He had frightened them. He didn't doubt that they intended to kill him when they had their information, so he had stalled, watching for a break.

They did not know his strength or agility. They had no idea of his skill with weapons and he had done nothing to lead them to believe he was anything more than a lawyer, a deskman.

He hadn't been taken in by Fanny Baston. She was beautiful, but there was something else about her, some unhealthy air that disturbed him. He had been careful.

Every step of the way he had been sure that no one was behind him, that he was always ready. He had not suspected his drink . . . not so soon.

Actually, although wary of trouble, he had not expected it. They were fishing to see what he knew, of that he was sure, and he suspected that when they decided he knew nothing they would bid him good night and that would be the end of it.

From the first, he had known that his mention of Pierre frightened them. Obviously, something had happened on that western expedition that they did not wish known. That in itself was peculiar because jurisdiction would be hard if not impossible to establish, witnesses impossible to obtain.

From the idle talk over dinner, before things became serious, he had heard Philip mentioned several times. And Philip, he gathered, was well-off. Philip had also been close to Pierre. Whether they were blood brothers he had not grasped, but it was clear that there was a bond of affection between them.

The knockout drops were unexpected. All had been casual. Andre was at the table . . . so were Paul and Fanny.

The drug was in the coffee, which was strong enough to cover the taste, and within a few minutes after he drank the coffee he realized he was in trouble. But by that time his movements were slowed, his coordination affected. He tried to get up, but Andre contemptuously shoved him back into his chair. The last thing he remembered was their faces as they sat around watching him with casual disinterest, almost boredom, as he faded out.

Something was happening. A boat bumped against the side of the houseboat and men came aboard. There was low argument, orders, men running. Suddenly the door to the hatchway descending into the hold where he lay was opened. A lantern held high found him with eyes closed. The hatch closed again, and he heard the bar drop.

He could only guess what was happening. Either they were leaving here or they were expecting someone, and it appeared to be the latter.

In the bilge there was a little black, dirty water slopping about. Several hours before, Orrin had worked loose one of the boards, then another. He had been soaking the rawhide that bound his wrists in this water, and the rawhide was slowly stretching. Already he could detect some looseness . . . just a little more.

Now he hooked a slightly loosened cord over a nail projecting from where he had removed the board, and he began to tug.

Sweat broke out on his forehead and his body. The rawhide cut deeply into his wrists, but he continued to work and strain. Nothing happened, but the rawhide did seem a little looser. Again he lay listening, his bound wrists in the water.

He could hear rats rustling somewhere forward. So far they had not come near him. Given time, they would.

Above, all was still. How many men were aboard? There had been two, but now there must be at least four, and they were waiting . . . waiting in the darkness, armed and ready.

It had to be Tell, of course.

If anybody was coming to help it had to be his brother, for there was no one else. Tyrel was far away in New Mexico, and none of the others were anywhere around as far as he knew.

Rousing himself, he strained against the rawhide. Then he hooked it over the nail again and chafed it against the nailhead.

The minutes passed. He worked, strained, tugged against the nail, and soaked the rawhide. He tried to turn his wrists inside the thongs, and they turned, ever so slightly.

Something furry brushed near him and he made a violent movement of repulsion. The rat went scurrying. He hooked the thong over the nail again and jerked and tugged. Suddenly, something gave. The strain on his wrists slackened. He shook his wrists, twisted them, and the thongs came free.

He brought his hands around in front of him. His wrists were raw and bloody, the cuffs on his shirt were blood-stained. He opened and closed his hands—they worked.

Swiftly, he went to work on his ankles. Topside all was still . . . he must remember that. In this quiet they could hear any unusual movement. He had no weapon, but he stood up slowly, making a noose of the rawhide. The piece from his ankles was all of five feet long. He tucked it into his belt and picked up one of the loose boards.

Not heavy. About six feet long and one by four inches. Not what he would like, but useful.

He stretched his muscles and moved closer to the hatch. There was a door, then four steps to the deck. He moaned . . . then again.

There was a stir topside. He grunted, thumped the deck, and then he heard soft footsteps. He heard fumbling with the hasp on the outside of the door, then a low call. "Hurry, Jake! Here they come!"

The door opened and the man with the lantern leaned forward and extended the lantern, peering into the dark hold.

With all the force he could muster, Orrin smashed him in the face with the end of the board, driving it with two hands, like a lance.

The man screamed and toppled over backward, his lantern falling, breaking, and spilling kerosene all over the steps. Flames sprang up, but Orrin leaped over them and lunged up the steps.

Somebody out on the water yelled, "Back off! Back off!" There was the roar of a shotgun. Orrin lifted the fallen man from the deck, slammed him against the bulkhead, and ripped a gun and a knife from his belt. He knocked the man sprawling and ran for the rail.

A huge man rushed around the corner and Orrin struck out with his fist, the fist that gripped the knife. The blow was wild, but it connected solidly, and he cut back and down with the blade. He felt cloth tear, heard a grunt of pain. A teeth-rattling blow caught him on the side of the head.

Orrin staggered, swung again, and then, knife still in hand, went over the rail into the water. Meanwhile, he was conscious of several gunshots, and a second bellow of the shotgun.

He came up in the dark water, felt the smack of a bullet on the water near him, then went under, turning at right angles. But he had seen the boat, and he struck out for it, swimming strongly.

His head came above water, and he said, "Tell!" in a low but carrying voice.

Instantly, the boat turned toward him. He dove, coming up on the far side. He grasped the gunwale of the boat. He saw the mast, several men, and light reflected on gun barrels. In the houseboat beyond, flames were leaping from the hatch and they could see men running with buckets, trying to put out the fire.

"Tell?" he whispered again.

"Orrin, damn you, when you get in be careful where you set. I got a new suit-coat folded on that seat, yonder."

Hands helped him in, and then the oar began, sculling the boat further away on the dark water.

Orrin's head still buzzed with the blow he had received, and the raw flesh on his wrists was stinging with salt from the water.

"Anybody got anything to drink? I haven't had a swallow since morning time."

Somebody handed him a bottle. He drank. "Burgundy," he said, "but a poor year."

"What happened to you?" I said. "You've been missing for days."

Orrin chuckled, drank again, and said, "Well, you see there was this girl—"

"I met her."

"I'll bet. But did you ever see that house she lives in? All white, with pillars yet, and great big oaks all around, and lawns, and—"

"What happened?" I repeated.

"We had a nice drink, and then dinner. By that time I wanted to return to the hotel. We had coffee and when I came out of it I was on that houseboat yonder and they were asking me questions about Colorado—about something hidden there.

"What could I tell them? All we're looking for is pa, but they wouldn't believe that. They beat me around a little, but not near as much as you did a few times back home when we were tussling. They figured on using some red-hot irons next time, so I decided it was time I left."

He drank again. "I've heard of southern hospitality, but this is going too far."

A little breeze came in from the sea and we hoisted our sail. I picked up my coat and held it in my lap.

Setting there in the boat, I listened to the low rumble of talk between the men. Somebody had warned the men on the houseboat and they had been waiting for us. Only the scream of the man Orrin hit had warned us. As it was, they had shot too soon when we were still only a shadow on the water, and their old-fashioned guns had scattered shot too quickly.

Despite our precautions, we had been followed. Somebody had seen us leave, and they had brought word to the houseboat by some shorter route through the bayous. Had Orrin made his break an instant later we'd have been within sight and range, and some of us, perhap all, would be feeding the fish and the 'gators.

"Tell," Orrin edged closer in the boat. "We've stirred up more than we know. There's been something lying quiet down here ever since pa disappeared, and we've upset the applecart."

"We'd better leave," I suggested. "It ain't worth getting killed over. Not just to find out what happened twenty years ago."

"Before we leave we'll make a call on Philip Baston. I think he could tell us something."

Well, we could do that, but I wanted to leave. New Orleans had always been a favorite town for me, but this time we just weren't likely to have much fun.

Yet what had happened those long years ago? And what did it have to do with us, and with pa? Somebody wanted to keep us from stirring muddy waters, but they also suspected we were here for some other purpose than hunting for pa.

Nobody was around when we tied our boat to the old dark wharf and came ashore. The Tinker and Tomas, the man in the striped shirt, walked along with us to the Saint Charles.

It was almost daybreak and there was nobody about, and I was just as pleased. Neither me nor Orrin looked like anybody you would expect to see at such an elegant hotel, but nobody saw us as we came in.

We'd slept maybe an hour when there was a discreet tapping on the door. It was Judas Priest.

"I've drawn a bath," he said, "and if you will, gentlemen, take no more time than you need. Meanwhile, I will brush and press your clothing."

"What's up?"

"The law," he said gently. "The law will wish to talk to you. I suggest you look and talk as innocently as possible. It is easier to get into prison here than to get out, and Andre Baston still has friends in town."

He took out his watch. "At best you have an hour. Probably less."

An hour later we were seated in the dining room, bathed, shaved, and combed. Our clothing was pressed, our manner calm. Each of us was reading a newspaper when the law came in.

CHAPTER VII

The man who approached our table was short, thickset, and dapper, but there was about him an air of competence, as Orrin said. He looked to me like a tough man to handle in a brawl.

He glanced at a paper in his hand. "Orrin and William T. Sackett?"

"That is correct, sir," Orrin said, folding his paper. "What can I do for you?"

"My name is Barres. I am a police officer."

Orrin smiled. "It is always a pleasure to meet another officer of the law."

Barres was surprised. "You're an officer?"

"An attorney, if you will. However, both my brother and myself have been marshals or deputy sheriffs out west."

"I was not aware of that. You are in town on business?"

"Legal business, actually." Orrin took a coffee cup from the next table and filled it from our coffeepot. "We are looking into the question of our father's death. It was some years ago, but there is an estate involved and we are doing our best to ascertain the facts."

"I see." Barres seemed to be searching for an approach. He looked at the cuts and bruises on Orrin's face. "What happened to you?"

"Let us put it this way, Mr. Barres, we do not intend to prefer charges unless charges are preferred against us."

Barres sipped some coffee. "There was some sort of a shooting on the river last night. Can you tell me anything about it?"

"Off the record, Mr. Barres, I was kidnapped, held in a houseboat on a bayou for several days, threatened often, and beaten several times. I escaped, and while I was escaping shots were fired."

"Could you identify any of those involved?"

"Certainly. I can identify almost all of them. And, if it comes to a matter of a trial, I can produce evidence as well as witnesses."

Barres was disturbed. He had come here under orders to make an inquiry and probably an arrest. Certain powers in the parish would prefer to have both Sacketts behind bars, and at once. They would also prefer to keep them there. Barres was not in favor of such tactics, but in the New Orleans of the seventies such things had been known to occur.

Furthermore, he had been told the Sacketts were a pair of thugs from Tennessee. For years most of the trouble along the river front had been caused by Kentucky or Tennessee boatmen, so arresting such men was quite in the usual order of business.

That they stayed at the Saint Charles was the first surprise, the second was their opulent appearance, the third that one of them was an attorney. Under the conditions, Barres being no fool, he chose to proceed cautiously.

"Might I ask where you make your home?"

"Santa Fe. Until recently I was a member of the legislature from New Mexico."

Worse and worse. Such men were not apt to be bluffing if they said they had evidence.

"Mr. Barres," Orrin suggested, "I came here to discover, if I could, who went west with my father. Almost at once I found difficulties arising that suggested to me that much more might be involved than simply locating the place of his death and burial.

"Now if this case goes to court it is going to create a scandal. It is going to cause considerable embarrassment to many people. We have one more call to make in New Orleans and then we expect to leave. To avoid trouble I suggest we be allowed to do just that.

"I have been in politics and I know that no political figure likes to be embarrassed or found supporting the wrong side. If such a thing occurs, he would have no kind thoughts about the officer who opened the whole Pandora's box."

"You're suggesting I drop the whole affair?"

"Yes. Within forty-eight hours we will be gone, and it is unlikely we will return to New Orleans for some time."

"Off the record, will you tell me about it?"

"Off the record, yes." Refilling his own cup, Orrin proceeded to outline the events of the past few days, beginning with his arrival in the city.

He named names, and he pulled no punches. "I suspect, Mr. Barres, that you are aware of the situation. These people are criminal of mind and intent; they are extremely dangerous because they believe themselves untouchable, but they are also amateurs.

"We wanted only information. We suspected nothing criminal. We wished to involve no one. All we wanted was the time of departure from New Orleans and the probable destination. I suspect that information could have been given to us by any of the Baston family."

"And suppose I were to arrest you now? This minute?"

Orrin smiled pleasantly. "Mr. Barres, I am sure you have no such intention. I believe you to be an honest man and a capable one. You are also intelligent enough to know that I am prepared for that eventuality.

"Two letters have been mailed. One before the arrival of my brother, another since the events of last night. If we do not contact my brother Tyrel in Mora within the next few days, he will initiate an investigation at the highest state level."

Barres chuckled. "Well, you don't forget much, do you? Also, off the record, Mr. Sackett, Andre Baston is a scalp-hunter. He's got a bloody record. Dueling is an old custom here. Usually, a little blood is drawn and that's the end of it . . . but not with Andre. He kills. I think he likes to kill."

"I've met the kind."

"What I am saying is, be careful. He may try to pick a quarrel now."

Orrin smiled. "Mr. Barres, my folks were feudal stock. We youngsters cut our teeth on gun butts. Tyrel and me, we crossed the plains in '66 and '67. If Andre Baston wants a fight, he has come to the right place to get it."

Barres shrugged. As I set there watching and listening, I knew that he, like many another man, was fooled by Orrin's easy-going manner. Orrin was an agreeable man, hard to annoy or offend, but hell on wheels in action.

"And the one man you wish to see?"

"Philip Baston. You may come with us, if you like."

"Me?" Barres was startled. "Mr. Sackett, you just don't understand. The only way I could get into Philip Baston's house is through the servants' entrance. If we had to arrest him for murder it would have to be done by the chief himself, along with the chief prosecuting officer. Philip Baston owns half a dozen sugar planta- tions, at least four ships sailing out of New Orleans, and a lot of buildings here in town. He's worth millions, but he's a gentleman, sir, a gentleman.

"He rarely leaves his home except to visit with an old friend or two or to supervise his properties. He contributes to charity, and he's ready to help with anything for the betterment of the city." Barres paused. "You may have trouble getting to see him."

After Barres took his leave, we finished our breakfast. It was nearly midday, and I couldn't recall a time in my life when I was still setting about the table at such an hour. Orrin, he done a part of his work that way, and usually had a book propped alongside him. Me, I was out yonder with a rope and a saddle and a bronc.

"Speaking of duels," Orrin said, "as the challenged party I would have the choice of weapons. A few years ago there was a member of the legislature down here who was seven feet tall—he'd been a blacksmith or something. He was challenged by a famous duelist who was much shorter. The big man did not want to fight, thought it useless, so he accepted the challenge and suggested sledgehammers, in six feet of water."

"What happened?"

"It amused the duelist so much he withdrew his challenge and the two became friends."

A carriage took us up the circular drive to the door. The house was a story and a half in height with six Doric columns across the front, the windows barred with wrought iron. Stretching out in front of the house as far as the bayou was a lawn scattered with huge old oaks trailing Spanish moss.

There were azaleas and camellias wherever we looked. It was a right fine place, and old.

Orrin sent in his card and we waited, seated in high-backed chairs the like of which I'd never seen. For my taste, there was kind of too much furniture in the room, me being used to Spanish ranch-house styles which were spacious, roomy, and cool.

We waited a few moments and then Philip Baston came in. He was a tall man, although not as tall as

Orrin or me, and slender. He glanced at both of us.
"I am Philip Baston. You wished to see me?"

"Sir," Orrin spoke quietly, "we do not wish to take
more of your time than need be, although I confess
there's a restfulness in this house that makes me wish
to prolong my stay.

"My brother, William Tell Sackett, and I are trying
to locate our father's grave. We understand he left here
with your brother-in-law, Pierre Bontemps, and we
thought you might be able to provide us with the
date and destination."

Philip Baston considered that, and then said briefly,
"Your father was known to Pierre through an ac-
quaintance who was killed. It was known that your
father was familiar with the San Juan Mountains in
Colorado, and Pierre asked him to act as a guide and to
share in the results, if any.

"They left here twenty years ago, almost to the day.
My brother-in-law and I were very close, gentlemen,
closer I might add, than I and my brother. He wrote to
me from Natchez, and another letter came from the
mouth of the Arkansas.

"I believe they went up the Arkansas from there to
Webber's Falls, but that is pure guesswork. From there
it was overland, but at that point they were together."

"Pierre Bontemps, my father, and—"

Philip Baston hesitated, and then said. "There were
four more at the time. My brother Andre, then a very
young man, a man named Pettigrew, and another
named Swan."

"*Hippo* Swan?" I asked.

Baston glanced at me. "Do you know the man?"

"He was pointed out to me."

He seemed about to say something further, then
turned back to Orrin. "There was one other . . . a
slave."

"His name?"

Again there was a moment of hesitation. "Priest.
Angus Priest."

Orrin got to his feet. "One thing more, sir, and then
we shall be on our way. What were they after?"

Baston looked disgusted. "They were hunting gold

buried by a French army detachment that mined it earlier. Supposedly this detachment was sent in there around 1790, and I believe there is some record of it.

"The reports vary, of course, but the consensus is that they dug some five million dollars in gold. The figure increases with each retelling of the story. I think Pierre and Andre believed the figure was closer to thirty million. In any event, from one cause or another the strength of the detachment was cut until a final Indian attack left only five of them to escape.

"Pierre had a map. Your father told him he could take him in to the location. So they started out."

"Thanks very much." Orrin thrust out his hand, and Philip took it. If he knew anything of our difficulties with his brother, he said nothing about it.

In the carriage we set quiet for a time, and then I said, "The gold could be there. There was many a place, them years, where a party of men could mine that much."

"Do you know the country?"

"Uh-huh. No city man's goin' to find anything up there, Orrin. That's almighty rough country, and she's high up. You've got a few months each year when a body can work, and then you have to hightail it out of there or get snowed in.

"Landmarks don't last in that high country, Orrin. There's heavy snow, wind, lightnin', an' rain. There's snowslides, landslides, and the passage of men and animals. Only the rocks last . . . for a while."

"What do you think about pa?"

"I think he took 'em to the hills. I think he took 'em high up yonder, and I think there was blood, Orrin. Andre and them, they're runnin' scared. Something happened only Andre knows of and the rest suspect."

"What could they be afraid of now? Us?"

"No, sir. Of Philip yonder. That's a fine, proud old man, and he has money. I think the rest of them hope to inherit, but likely he doesn't approve of them, and if he found some cause to suspect what happened to Pierre, well, they'd have nothing."

"I think they have some notion of going for the gold."

"Likely."

"What do you think we should do?"

"I think we should catch ourselves a steamer, Orrin, and go back upriver hunting folks with long memories. There's always one, a-settin' by somewheres who'll recall. We want a man who can recall."

"Tomorrow?"

"I reckon. First, though, I've got a little something to do. I'm going to have a little quiet talk with a priest."

CHAPTER VIII

We packed our gear in the morning, and we booked our passage north, and as much as I liked that wonderful, colorful town, I was ready to hit for the high country again. I wanted to see the wide plains with the mountains in the purple haze yonder, and I wanted to feel a good horse under me and ride out where the long wind bends the grass.

First I had to talk to a priest—a Judas Priest. And he was nowhere in sight, nor to be found wherever I looked. He'd quit his hotel job. They spoke well of him, although they looked at me strangely when I asked after him, and they commented that he was an odd one.

"What do you mean—odd?" Orrin asked.

The man just shrugged and would say nothing, but I wasn't going to leave it at that, so I caught up with another porter I'd seen around and I took out a couple of silver dollars, tossed them and ketched them.

When I asked my question he looked at me and at those dollars. "He took to you, mister. He done tol' me so. He thought there was a charm on you. He thought you walked well with the spirits, mister. He said you follered the right, and the evil would never come to you."

"Where will I find him?"

"If'n he wishes to be found, he'll find you. Don't

you look, mister. He's voodoo, he is. Pow'ful strong voodoo."

Well, no matter what he was, I wanted to talk with him. The slave who had gone west with Pierre Bontemps had been named Angus Priest, and I had a hunch there was more than one reason behind the help Judas had provided.

We saw nothing of Andre Baston, nor of the others. I had an urge to go hunting Hippo Swan, but I fought it down. We'd promised Barres we'd leave and take the ache from his thoughts, so we done it, but I left not thinking kindly of Hippo.

The river was a busy place them days. We took a stateroom called the Texas, the highest point on a riverboat except the pilothouse. It was said along the river that Shreve, for whom Shreveport was named, had named cabins for the various states, and ever after they were called staterooms.

Now I've no knowledge of the language or anything. I'm a fair hand with a rope and a horse, with some know-how about cattle and reading sign, but words kind of interest me, and many a time I've covered miles out yonder where there's nothing but grass and sky, just figuring on how words came to be. Like Dixie Land. For a time they issued a ten-dollar note down there in New Orleans that had a *ten* on one side and a *dix*— French for ten—on the other. Folks began calling them *dixies*, and the word somehow got to mean the place they were used—Dixie Land.

At the last minute the Tinker showed up and wanted to go along with us, so the three of us headed north for the Arkansas. The Tinker showed for dinner in a perfectly tailored black suit, looking almighty elegant like some foreign prince, which among his own folks he probably was.

We set up to table, hungry as all get-out. We were giving study to the card on which they'd printed what grub was available when a soft voice said, "Something from the bar, gentlemen?" It was Judas Priest.

"I have been wanting to talk to you," I said.

He smiled with sly amusement. "Ah? Of course. I shall be available later." He paused a moment. "If you gentlemen do not object, and could use some good cooking on your way west, I would be pleased to accompany you."

"Can you ride?"

He smiled again. "Yes, suh. I can ride. And to answer your question, suh," he looked at me, "I look for a grave as well as you. I also look for the reason why there needs to be a grave."

"Come along, then," Orrin replied. "And we'll take you up on the cooking."

It was midnight, a few days later, when we transferred from our upriver steamer to the smaller steamer that would take us up the Arkansas. Judas, in his mysterious way, had transferred too, refusing any assistance from us.

Orrin went to his cabin, and I loitered on deck, watching the lights of the big steamer as it pulled away, churning the water to foam as it made the turn. In the waves thrown up by the paddle wheels there was a boat, a small boat that seemed to have appeared from the other side of the steamer. I watched it idly, but it was dark after the steamer's lights and I could make out nothing. A little later I heard the dip and splash of oars. The boat was pulling in alongside a keelboat moored below us.

It seemed to me that two men, perhaps three, left the boat. I was tired now, and walked slowly forward to our cabin.

The Tinker moved from the shadow of some barrels. "Did you see that boat?"

"Yes."

"Somebody could have gotten off on the river side."

"You're a suspicious man, Tinker."

"I am a living man, my friend."

We stood together in the darkness watching the water as our small steamer got underway. If we did not get aground too often we'd soon be riding out for Colorado. Yet river travel was a chancy thing, subject to sudden lows or highs along the river, unexpected sand bars, snags, and all drifting matter. A pilot had to be a bit of a magician to do it well, and navigating these branches of the Big River was doubly difficult. Nor did they dare to go too far upstream for they might suddenly be left high and dry as a sudden flood played out.

"Your pa, now. You never heard anything after New Orleans?" said the Tinker.

"We never heard from him from there that I recall, but my memory is hazy, and it wasn't long after that before I took off to make my way in the world. Then the war came along and blotted a lot of memories for us who fought."

We were silent for a while, listening to the river whispering along the hull. There was a light on that keelboat downstream now.

"When somebody is around home there's talk, and the talk awakens memories, so a body has many a thing fresh in mind that otherwise might fade out.

"There are sons and daughters of the same folks who have altogether different memories, and each one thinks he remembers better. The last one at home, of course, has had his memories renewed by talk. I suspect Orrin or Tyrel would recall better than me. Especially Tyrel. He never forgets anything."

"Your pa may have been murdered."

"Maybe."

"I don't like the feel of it, Tell. There's something that doesn't feel right about it," he said.

"Could be Andre took off and left them in a bind—pulled out—and he's shamed Philip may find out and cut them off. From all I could gather, Andre, Paul, and Fanny have gone through everything they have. They're in a tight for cash, and they've got to set right with Philip or go to work."

"There's more to it," said the Tinker and went in to the cabin.

There was some stirring around on the keelboat aft of us. I didn't pay it much mind, only to notice.

The river rustled by our hull. The deck below was piled high with cargo. I'd seen these riverboats so piled with bales of cotton that folks in the cabins had to live by candlelight even at midday. That water down there had melted from high-mountain snows not long since.

It had trickled down, pure and cold from up where the glaciers still live, where the rivers are born.

Soon I'd be riding where that water came from. Here it was muddy with earth, with death and plants and bugs, and with whatever man left in it. Far up there where the snows were the water was pure and cold.

No getting away from it, I was wilderness born and bred and never was I wishful to be far from it. I like to bed down where a man can look up at the stars, where he can taste the wind to test the weather, and where he can watch the wild things about their business.

When a man lives with the wilderness he comes to an acceptance of death as a part of living, he sees the leaves fall and rot away to build the soil for other trees and plants to be born. The leaves gather strength from sun and rain, gathering the capital on which they live to return it to the soil when they die. Only for a time have they borrowed their life from the sum of things, using their small portion of sun, earth, and rain, some of the chemicals that go into their being—all to be paid back when death comes. All to be used again and again.

Feet rustled on the deck behind me, a swift movement, and on instinct I squatted quickly, turned and lifted with all the thrust of my legs into an upward drive. I felt legs across my back and shoulders, then the weight slid off me and over the rail into the water.

He'd been wet before he fell, which meant that he probably swam over, crawled up on the deck, and came at me from behind with a knife or a club. He'd jumped at me, and when I dropped he just carried right on over, helped a mite by my boost.

He went down a long way because we were a far piece above the water, and when he came up I called down, "How's the water there, son?"

He made reply, but it sounded almighty unpleasant, so I just turned about and went to our cabin. Orrin was asleep, and so was the Tinker.

I shucked my coat and boots, took my gun close to hand, and peeled to my long-johns. I stretched out on the bunk and looked up into the blackness. It was going to be all right. I was headed back for the mountains . . .

When the little steamer tied up at Webber's Falls, we were the first ones down the gangplank. "They're in town," I told Orrin and the Tinker. "Walk easy and keep your eyes open. You boys get us some grub and supplies at the store. I'll wait for Judas and then try to find some horses."

When Judas came off the boat I told him to meet us at the store later and to watch himself.

There was a livery stable and a corral down the street. Strolling along, I stopped and leaned on the rails. A man with a straw hat and bib overalls came over to me. "Nice stock," he commented.

There were a dozen horses in the corral; all but two would be useless to us. Two were farm animals, the rest Indian ponies. The other horses, the two I fancied above the rest, were still not what I wanted.

"Not for me," I shook my head. "Isn't there anything better around?"

"Well," he said, "there's a man with a ranch the other side of town. His name is Halloran, Doc Halloran. He buys cattle, sells them, buys horses, races them. He's got fine stock but he ain't in the trading business."

He hired me a rig and I stopped by the store. When I explained what I was about, the Tinker said, "Doc Halloran, you say? I'll go along."

Orrin was still buying, so we drove off.

It was an interesting place. A log house of five or six rooms, a handsome big barn, corrals, a well, some hay meadows, and a green lawn in front of the house.

A tall, lean man came from the house as we drove up. A couple of Indian cowhands were at the corral.

I started to speak, but the tall man was looking past me at the Tinker. A broad smile broke over his face. "Tinker! Well, I'll be forever damned!"

"I hope not, Doc. Good to see you. This is Tell Sackett."

"Where's Lando? Is he still fighting?" He turned to me. "Are you kin to Lando? He won me more money than I ever won anywhere else. Fight? That's the fightin'est man who ever walked."

"He's my cousin," I said. "We Sacketts run to boys and fighting."

"Come in! Come in! By the lord harry, this is great! Tinker, I've often wondered what became of you. Figured you must have gone back to pack-peddling in the mountains. What brings you to the Falls?"

"Headed west," I said, "and we heard you had some horses that weren't for sale. We also heard they were the best stock anywhere around."

"How many d'you need?"

"Three packhorses, four head of riding stock, and we want stayers."

"I've got what you need. A few years back, just after I moved up here from Oakville where I met Lando an' the Tinker, I swapped for an appaloosa stallion. A half-breed Injun from up Idaho way rode him into town. On the dodge, I reckon.

"Well, I bred that appaloosa to some Morgan mares I had here, and wait until you see 'em!" He stopped suddenly, looking from one to the other. "You boys ain't runnin' from something, are you?"

"No. Kind of scouting my father's trail," I explained. "Is there anybody around who was here twenty years ago? Somebody who might have outfitted another party with horses?"

"More than likely they outfitted at Fort Gibson, right up the line. Those days nobody stopped here very much. This place was started by a part-blood Creek who came in here a good many years back. He took over the salt-works up the stream. Did right well. But anybody outfitting for the western ride would go to Fort Gibson."

We finished our coffee and got up. "Let's see those horses," I suggested. "We've got to get back to town. Orrin will be waiting."

There were three of them, sixteen hands, beautifully built, and in fine shape. One was a gray with a splash of white with black spots on the right shoulder, and a few spots freckled over the hips, black amidst the gray. The other horses were both black with splashes

of white on the hips and the usual spots of the appaloosa.

"We'll take them. How about packhorses?"

"There," he indicated a dun, a pinto, and a buckskin.
"They're good stock themselves, mustang cross."

"How much?"

He laughed. "Take 'em and forget it. Look, when
Lando Sackett whupped Dunc Caffrey down to Oakville
I went down for all I had, and with my winnings I
bought this place and my stock. I built it up and I still
have money in the bank.

"Take 'em along, an' welcome. Only thing is, if
Lando fights again, you write me. I'll come a-runnin'."

"Thanks," I said, "but—"

"No buts." Doc Halloran shook his head at me.
"Forget it.

"Reason I asked was you on the dodge," he said,
"because three hard cases drifted in a few days ago.
They've been sort of hangin' around as if on the lookout
for somebody."

The Tinker looked at me, and me at him. Then we
sprinted for the buckboard.

CHAPTER IX

Orrin didn't make it sound like much when he told
us of it after. He was in that there store, and it was
like most country stores, smelling of everything that was
in it—good, rich, wonderful smells of new leather,
fresh-ground coffee, cured hams and bacon, spices, and
the like.

He knew where we were going and how we'd have to
live. We'd have fresh meat from the country around us,
and we'd have what we could gather in the way of roots
and such, only that wouldn't amount to much unless we
happened on it.

A man traveling doesn't have much time for stopping
off to look or pick, so Orrin was buying sides of bacon,

flour, meal, coffee, dried fruit, and whatever figured to be handy.

He also was buying some .44's for our Winchesters and pistols, and the man who owned the store took down a spanking new Smith and Wesson .44 and was showing it to Orrin.

Orrin had just put it down when those hard cases walked in. Now they weren't from the western lands, they were river men, mean as all get-out, but they didn't know Orrin. They'd been told they were to kill a lawyer . . . now there's lawyers and there's lawyers.

Just like there was a dentist named Doc Holiday.

They came in the store at the front, and Orrin was back yonder at the counter. He must have turned to look, as he would, but likely he was expecting the Tinker an' me.

Now those three spread out a little after they got through the door, and they were all looking at him. It was three to one, and Orrin spoke to the storekeeper out of the corner of his mouth. "You better get out. This appears to be a shooting matter."

"You know those men?"

"No, but they look like they're hunting."

One of them, who wore a tall beaver hat, noticed the gun on the counter. He had his in his hand. He smiled past some broken, yellowed teeth and a straggly mustache.

"There it is, mister lawyer. You better try for it."

Now that gun was brand new and empty. Orrin knew that, even if they didn't. He could also see these were river men, and while there'd been a sight of shooting and killing along the Mississippi, very little of it was based on fast drawing.

"If I reached for that gun, you'd kill me."

The man with the beaver hat gave him a wolfish grin. "I reckon."

"But if I don't reach for it, you'll kill me anyway?"

"I reckon we'll do that, too." He was enjoying himself.

"Then I haven't much choice, have I?"

"Nope. You sure ain't."

The other two men were shifting, one to get far over

on his left. One of them was momentarily behind some
bib overalls hung from a rafter.

"But if I don't want to reach for that gun, how about
this?"

As Orrin spoke, he drew and fired.

Reaction time was important. The three would-be
killers were sure that he was frightened, that being a
lawyer he would not be a gunfighter, and that if he
reached it would be for the gun on the counter.

Orrin had always been quick. And he was a dead
shot. He fired and turned sharply to bring the second
man in line, when there was the bellow of a shotgun
behind him. The man farthest right cried out and ran
for the door. He blundered into the doorpost and then
almost fell through the screen door in getting out, a
growing circle of blood on his back and shoulder.

The third man, who had been moving toward the left,
dropped his gun and lifted his hands. "Don't shoot! For
God's sake, *don't shoot!*"

Orrin held his gun ready. "All right," he said quietly,
"move toward the door. Your friend out there may
need some help."

The man gestured toward the one with the beaver
hat, who had a blue hole between his eyes. "What about
him?"

"Take him out and bury him. Then if you want to
kill somebody, go get the man who set you up for this."

"They said you was a lawyer!"

"I am. But out where I come from every butcher,
baker, and candlestick maker has used a gun. Besides,
haven't you ever heard of Temple Houston? He is old
Sam Houston's boy, and a lawyer, too, but a dead shot.
It doesn't pay to take anything for granted."

The man left, and Orrin turned to the storekeeper.
"Thanks, friend. Thanks, indeed."

The old man was brusque. "Don't thank me, young
man. I can't have folks comin' in here shootin' at my
customers. It's bad for business."

That was the way it set when our buckboard came
a hellin' down the street from Doc Halloran's place. We
saw a man lyin' bloody on the boardwalk and another
kneelin' by him.

The Tinker and me unlimbered from that buckboard and the kneeling man looked up. "Don't go in there, fellers. That lawyer in there's hell on wheels."

"It'll be all right," I said. "I'm his brother."

"Who put you up to it?" the Tinker asked.

"A couple of dudes. We was to get fifty dollars a piece for you two. That's a sight of money, mister."

Orrin came through the door. "How much is it to your dead friend inside?" he asked.

The man stared from him to me.

"What about those dudes who hired you?" I said. "Two young men?"

"No, sir. A young man and a woman. Looked to be brother and sister."

"In New Orleans?"

"No, sir. In Natchez-under-the-Hill."

Orrin looked at me. "They are following us, then."

The man looked up. "Mister, would you help me get this man to a doctor?"

A bystander said, "We've no doctor here. The storekeeper usually fixes folks up when they're hurt."

"Him?" The man on his knees looked bleak. "He already done fixed him once."

Orrin spoke more quietly. "My friend, I am sorry for you. You were just in the wrong line of work, but if you'll take a closer look, your friend has just run out of time."

And it was so. The man on the ground was dead.

Slowly, the man got up. He wiped his palms on his pants. He was young, not more than twenty-two, but at the moment he was drawn and old. "What happens now? Does the law want me?"

Someone standing there said, "You just leave town, mister. We don't have any law here. Just a graveyard."

Judas came along when the shooting was all over, and we stayed the night at Halloran's. In the morning, once more in the saddle, we started west.

Four of us riding west, two from Tennessee, a gypsy, and a black man, under the same sun, feeling the same wind. We rode through Indian territory, avoiding villages, avoiding the occasional cattle herds, wanting only to move west toward the mountains.

We cut over the Rabbit Ear Creek country toward Fort Arbuckle. This was Creek Indian country. The land was mostly grass with some patches of timber here and there, mostly blackjack of white oak with redbud growing in thick clumps along the creeks.

We had grub enough, so we fought shy of folks, watched our back trail, and moved along about thirty miles or so each day. Arbuckle had been deserted by the army, but there were a few Indians camped there, trading horses and such. They were a mixed lot, Seminoles, Choctaws, and Creeks mostly, with a few Pottawattomies. We bought some coffee from them, and I traded for a beaded hunting shirt tanned almost white, a beautiful job.

"Be careful," a Creek warned us, "the Comanches have been raiding south and west of here. They ran off some horses only a few miles west."

Glancing around at Judas, I asked, "Can you shoot?"

"I can, suh."

Well, that was enough for me. He was no spring chicken but the first time I seen him top off a bronc I knew he'd been there before. He told me he could ride and he could, so when he told me he could shoot, I believed him.

As we rode out of Arbuckle and headed west up the Washita, I dropped back beside him. "Do you know any more about what happened than we do?"

"I doubt it, suh. Angus was slave to Mr. Pierre. Angus liked him, and Mr. Pierre was both a gentleman and a kind man. Angus was of an adventurous spirit, suh. He was a fine hunter and a man who liked the wilderness."

"Did you talk to him after plans were made to go west?"

"Once, only. He had met Mr. Sackett, your father, and liked him. Your father had very kindly advised him as to what he might encounter, the best clothing, and as to caution in all things.

"May I also say, suh, that he did not like Mr. Swan,

and none of us cared for Andre Baston. Do not mistake it, suh, Mr. Baston is a very dangerous man."

We saw occasional antelope, and twice we encountered small herds of buffalo, but we did not hunt. This was Indian country and for the moment we did not need meat. We neither wanted to shoot their game, for this was on land allotted to them, nor to attract attention to us from wild Indians.

Several times we cut their sign. Comanches . . . at least a dozen riding together.

"Raiders," Orrin said, and I agreed. Only warriors, no women, no travois.

This was all Indian country, about half wild and half friendly, and the friendly Indians suffered as much from the wild ones as the white men would. It was the old story of nomadic peoples raiding the settlements, and it has happened the world over.

Our camps at night were hidden, meals hastily prepared, and the fires kept to coals or to nothing at all. Judas proved an excellent camp cook, which pleased me. I could cook but didn't favor it much, and Orrin was no better than me. As for the Tinker, he kept silent on the subject.

We were coming up to the site of old Fort Cobb when Orrin, who was riding point, suddenly pulled up. A horse nickered, and then a dozen Indians rode over the crest of the hill.

Sighting us they pulled up sharp, but I held my hand up, palm out, as a signal we were peaceful, and they rode up.

They were Cheyennes, and they had been hunting along Cache Creek. By the look of things they had been successful, for they were loaded down with meat.

They warned us of a war party of Kiowas over west and south and swapped some meat with us for some sugar. We sat our horses and watched them go, and I suggested we swing north.

For the next few days we switched directions four or five times, riding north to Pond Creek, following it for a day or so, then a little south to confuse anybody following us, and finally north toward the Antelope Hills and the Texas Panhandle.

This was open grass country with a few trees along
the water courses, but little enough timber even there.
We picked up fuel where we could find it during the
day, and at night gathered buffalo chips. We were heading into empty country where there would be almost no
water.

We came suddenly upon a group of some twenty
horses, all unshod, traveling northwest by north. I
pulled rein.

"Indians," I said.

The Tinker glanced at me. "Might they not be wild
horses?"

"Uh-uh. If they were wild horses, you'd find a pile
of dung, but you see it's scattered along and that means
the Indians kept their horses in motion.

"The tracks are two days old," I added, "and were
made early in the morning."

The Tinker was amused, but curious, too. "How
do you figure that?"

"Look," I said, "there's sand stuck to those blades
of grass that were packed down by the horses' hooves
—over there, too. See? There hasn't been any dew for
the past two mornings, but three days ago there was
a heavy dew. That's when they passed by here."

"Then we don't have to worry," he suggested.

I chuckled. "Suppose we meet them coming back?"

We rode on, holding to shallow ground when we
could find it. We were now coming into an area that
undoubtedly has some of the flattest land on earth—
land cut by several major canyons. However, those
canyons were, I believed, much to the south of us.

I was pretty sure we were following much the same
route pa would have taken in coming west. We'd
switched around here and there, but nonetheless I believed our general route to be the one he would have
followed twenty years before.

Their needs for water and fuel would have been the
same as ours, and their fears of Indians even greater
since this had been entirely Indian country in their
time. The times when I'd traveled wilderness country
with pa had been few, mostly in the mountains, when
I was a very young boy. Yet I knew how his thinking

went, for he had given us much of our early education, either by the fireside or out in the hills. He was a thinking man, and he had little enough to leave us aside from the almost uncanny knowledge of wilderness living that he had picked up over the years.

No man likes to think of all he has learned going up like the smoke of a fire, to be lost in the vastness of sky and cloud. Pa wanted to share it with us, to give us what he learned, and I listened well, them days, and I learned a sight more than I guessed.

So when we saw that knoll with the flat rocks atop it and the creek with trees growing along it, I said to Orrin, "About there, Orrin. I'd say about there."

"I'll bet," he agreed.

"What is it?" Judas inquired.

"That's the sort of place pa would camp, an' if I ain't mistaken, that there's McClellan Creek."

CHAPTER X

We spurred our horses and loped on up to the edge of a valley maybe a mile wide. There were large cottonwoods along the banks of a mighty pretty stream that was about twenty feet wide but no more than six inches deep.

The water was clear and pure, coming down from the Staked Plain that loomed above and to the west of us. None of us relished that ride, but we had it to do.

"Marcy named this stream after McClellan," Orrin said. "He believed McClellan was the first white man to see it. Marcy was exploring the headwaters of the Red and the Canadian rivers on that trip."

"We'll camp," I said.

We scouted the stream for the best location for a camp and found it at a place where a huge old cottonwood had toppled to the ground. The upper branches and some leaves that still clung to them were in the water, but the trunk of the tree made a good break from the wind, and the other cottonwoods shaded the place. There was a kind of natural corral where we could bunch the horses.

First we staked them out to graze. The Tinker set watch over them whilst Judas whipped up the grub.

Orrin and me, we nosed around.

The way we figured, we were right on pa's old trail, and we were wishful of looking about to see if he left sign. Now all men have their patterns of using tools, making camp, and the like. Time had swept away most things a man might leave behind, and this was a country of cold and heat with hard winds and strong rains coming along all too often.

This was likely a camp where they'd spend time. A long trek was behind them, the Staked Plain before them, and they knew what that meant.

It was a snug camp. When the horses had grazed enough on the bottom grass, the Tinker brought them in and we settled them down in the corral.

A man riding wild country keeps his eyes open for camping places. He may not need one at that spot on the way out, but it might be just what the doctor ordered on the way back. Camps, fuel, defensive positions, water, landmarks, travel-sign . . . a man never stops looking.

We'd traveled steady, if not fast, and we'd lost time here and there trying to leave nothing an Indian would care to follow, yet I was uneasy. Too many attempts had been made to do away with us, and it wasn't likely we'd gotten off scot-free.

Leaving camp, I wandered off upstream toward where the creek came down from under the cap rock. It was good sweet water and there wasn't much of that hereabouts, for most of the streams were carrying gypsum, or salts, or something of the kind.

Andre Baston had evidently been with the party when it reached here, so he would know of this water and would come to it. How many he would have with him I wouldn't be able to guess, but he would pick up some hard cases along the way and he'd be prepared for trouble.

The feel of the country isn't right, and something inside tells me, warns me. What is it? Instinct? But what is instinct? Is it the accumulation of everything I've ever seen or smelled tickling a little place in my memory?

This is the kind of place I like. It is one of those lonely, lovely places you have to go through hell to reach. Many a man's home is just that, I expect.

Thin water running over sand—water so clear the whole bottom is revealed to you, and even a track left an hour ago may still be there . . . like *that* one.

The track of a horse, and beyond it another. I waded the stream, following them.

A slight smudge of a hoof on the grassy bank, tracks going away toward the cliffs. I was careful not to let my eyes look that way, but turned and strolled casually along the stream bank for thirty or forty yards, and then I walked back to camp.

I stopped twice on the way back. Once to pick up some sticks for fuel, another time to look at a place where a rabbit had been sleeping. At camp I dropped the fuel.

Orrin had gone off downstream, and I had to get him back.

"Tracks," I told them. "Get your rifles and keep a careful eye open all around. That was a shod horse, so they're here—or somebody is."

"How old was that track?" the Tinker wondered.

"Hour—maybe more. That water's not running so fast. It isn't carrying much silt, so it's hard to say. A track like that will lose its shape pretty fast, so I'd surmise not over an hour, and we've been here about half that time—maybe more.

"My guess would be they've seen us coming and they figured we wouldn't pass up a good camp spot like this. I think they are out there now . . . waiting."

I took my Winchester, and I shoved two handfuls of shells into my pockets. I was already wearing a cartridge belt, every loop loaded.

"Take nothing for granted. They may wait until night and they may come just any time." Thinking about it, I said, "Make out to be collecting fuel, but sort of pick up around. Get everything packed except grub and the frying pan. We may move suddenlike."

The brush was thicker downstream, and there were more cottonwoods and willows. A few paths ran away through the brush—deer, buffalo, and whatnot. Moving out, I hung my Winchester over my shoulder by its sling, just hanging muzzle down from my left shoulder, my left hand holding the barrel. A lift of the left hand, the muzzle goes up, the butt comes down, and the right hand grabs the trigger guard. With practice, a man can get a rifle into action as quickly as a six-gun.

Thick blackberry brush, some willows, and some really big cottonwoods. Orrin's tracks were there, and then Orrin.

He turned when he saw me coming. "Whatever happened, must have happened *there*—in the mountains, I mean, or on the way back."

"You think they found the gold?"

"Found it, or sign of it," he said. "Maybe it was late in the season before they located anything, and all of a sudden Andre or Pierre or somebody suddenly got the idea they should have it all."

"Andre got back, and Hippo Swan. They must have been the youngsters of the group."

Quietly then, I told him of the horse tracks and my feeling about them. We started back toward camp, taking our time and returning by a somewhat different route. We were only a few hundred yards downstream, but I'd caught no pattern to Andre's thinking, so I'd no way of knowing how he might choose to attack.

He was a fighting man, that much I knew, and I gathered that he'd not step back from murder. He didn't strike me as a man of honor, and from what I'd heard of his dueling and of his approach to LaCroix, I figured him to be a man to take any advantage.

"Orrin, there's no use in setting by an' lettin' him choose his time. Besides, we're lookin' to find what happened to pa, not to have a shoot-out with Andre Baston."

"What are you suggesting?"

"That come nightfall we Injun out of here, back south for the Red, follow it right up the canyon as far as we can go, then take off across the Staked Plains for Tucumcari or somewhere yonder."

We left our fire burning where the grass wouldn't catch, and we Injuned out of there, holding to the brush until it was fairly dark, then heading off to the south. For four mounted men with packhorses we moved fast and light and made mighty little sound.

By sunup we were twenty miles off, following along the route McClellan had taken in 1852. We camped, rested an hour or two, then turned west across the plains toward the canyon of the Red.

Finally the sandy bottom of the stream played out and the water was sweet where it ran over rock. The last tributaries must have been bringing the gypsum into the water.

We found a trail where a steep climb and a scramble would get us out of the canyon and we took off across country. I knew about where Tucumcari Mountain lay, a good landmark for old Fort Bascom. Twice we made dry camp, and once we found a spring. We stopped again when we met a sheepman who provided us with tortillas and frijoles. Our horses were taking a beating, so when we spotted a herd of horses and some smoke, we came down off the mesa and cut across the desert toward them.

Orrin eased his horse closer to mine. "I don't like the look of it," he said. "That's no ordinary bunch of stock."

We slowed down to come up to the herd at a walk. We saw four men: three hard-looking white men and a Mexican with twin bandolier loaded with rifle cartridges. They were set up as if for a fight.

"Howdy!" I said affably. "You got any water?"

The sandy-haired white man jerked his head toward some brush. "There's a seep." He was looking at our horses. Hard-ridden as they were, they still showed their quality. "Want to swap horses?"

"No," Orrin said, "just a drink and we'll drift."

As we rode by I glanced at the brands, something any stockman will do as naturally as clearing his throat. At the seep I swung my horse, facing them. "Orrin, you an' the Tinker drink. I don't like this outfit."

"See those brands?" he said. "That's all full-grown stock, but there isn't a healed brand in the lot."

"They've just worked them over," I agreed. "They'll hold them here until they're healed, then drift them out of the country."

"There's some good stock there," the Tinker said. "Some of the best."

When Orrin and the Tinker were in the saddle, I stepped down with Judas Priest. He drank, and then me, and as I got up from the water, Orrin said, "Watch it, boy," to me.

They were coming toward us.

I waited for them. They didn't know who we were, but they had an eye for our horses, all fine stock although ganted down from hard riding over rough country.

"Where you from?" asked the sandy-haired man.

"Passin' through," I replied mildly, "just passin' through."

"We'd like to swap horses," he said. "You've good stock. We'll swap two for one."

"With a bill of sale?" I suggested.

He turned sharp on me. He had a long neck, and when he turned like that he reminded me of a turkey buzzard. "What's that mean?"

"Nothin'," I replied mildly. "On'y my brother here, he's a lawyer. Likes to see things done proper."

He glanced at Orrin, wearing several days' growth of beard, his clothes dusty. "I'll bet!" he sneered.

"Better fill your canteens," I told Judas. "We may make a dry camp tonight."

"All right, Mr. Sackett," he said.

The sandy-haired man jerked as if slapped. "What was that? *What* did you call him?"

"Sackett," Judas said.

The other men backed off now, spreading out a little. The sandy-haired man's face was pale. "Now, see here," he said. "I'm just drivin' these horses across country. Hired by a man," he said nervously. "We were hired to drive these horses."

"Where's the man who hired you?"

"He's comin' along. There's a bunch of them. They'll be along directly."

"What's his name?" Orrin demanded suddenly.

The man hesitated. "Charley McCaire," he said finally.

Orrin glanced at me. McCaire was a gunfighter, a man with a reputation as a troublemaker, but one who so far had always kept on the good side of the law. He ranched in Arizona now, but he had several brothers who still lived in New Mexico and Texas.

"Orrin," I said, "keep an eye on these boys. I'm going to ride over and have a better look at those horses."

"Like hell you are!" the man said harshly. "You leave that herd alone!"

"Sit quiet," Orrin advised. "We're just wondering why the name Sackett upset you so."

Well, I trotted my appaloosa over to those horses and skirted around them a couple of times, then I bunched them a mite and rode back.

"Blotted," I said, "and a poor job. They read *888* and they should read *Slash SS*."

"Tyrel's road brand," Orrin said. "Well, I'll be damned!"

CHAPTER XI

The man's face was tight. "Now, you see here!" he said. "I—"

"Shut up," Orrin said sternly. His eyes went from one face to the other. "As of this moment you are all under arrest. I am making a citizen's arrest. Under the circumstances, if you do not offer resistance, I may be able to save you from hanging."

"We'll see about that!" the sandy-haired man yelled angrily. "You talk to Charley McCaire! And there he comes!"

Judas and the Tinker had spread out a little, facing the cattle drivers. Orrin an' me, we just naturally turned around to face the riders coming up to us. There were seven in the group, and a salty-looking bunch they were.

McCaire was a big man, rawboned and strong. Once you had a look at him you had no doubt who was in command. A weathered face, high cheekbones, and a great beak of a nose above a tight, hard mouth and a strong jaw.

"What the hell's goin' on here?" he demanded.

"Mr. McCaire? I am Orrin Sackett. I have just made an arrest of these men, found with stolen horses."

"*Stolen* horses?" McCaire's voice was harsh. "Those horses carry my brand."

"Every brand is blotted," I said calmly. "Three Eights over a Slash SS. That's Tyrel Sackett's road brand."

Now a man expecting trouble had better not miss anything. To the right of McCaire, there was a younger man with lean, flashy good looks about him—one of those men you sometimes see who just doesn't seem to hang together, and he was acting a mite itchy and tight around the mouth.

As I looked, his horse sort of fidgeted around, and I saw that gent's hand drop to his gun.

"*McCaire!* You tell that man to get his hand off his gun! There needn't be any shooting here, but if he wants it, he can have it."

McCaire's head swiveled around and his voice rapped like a gavel. "Get your hand off that gun, Boley!" He turned to the rest of his men. "Nobody starts shooting here until I do! *Get that?*"

Then he turned his eyes back to me, and, brother, those eyes of his, cold gray against his dark, wind-burned features, looked into me like a couple of gun muzzles. "Who're you?"

"William Tell Sackett's the name. Brother to Orrin here, and to Tyrel, whose horses these are."

"Those ain't nobody's horses but Charley's," Boley said.

Orrin ignored him. "Mr. McCaire, you're known as a hard man but a fair one. You can read brands as well as any man . . . and those are raw brands, Mr. McCaire, and there isn't a horse in that lot under four years old, nor are they mustangs. Such horses would have been branded long since."

McCaire turned in the saddle to an older man near him. "Tom, let's go have a look." He said to the others, "You boys just sit your saddles and don't start anything."

Orrin started to ride off with them and glanced at me. I grinned at him. "I'll just sort of sit here, too, Orrin. No reason these boys should get lonesome."

Boley looked past me at Judas, then at the Tinker. "Who are them?" he demanded. "What kinda people are you, anyhow?"

The Tinker smiled, flashing his white teeth, his eyes faintly ironic. "I'm a gypsy, if you'd enjoy knowing, and they call me the Tinker. I fix things," he added. "I put things together to make them work, but I can take them apart, too." He took his knife from its scabbard. "Sometimes I take things apart so they never work again." He dropped the knife back to its sheath.

Judas said nothing, merely looking at them, his eyes steady, his hands still.

Charley McCaire was at the horses now, him and that segundo of his. He would be able to see those were blotted brands, but a whole lot depended on whether he wanted to see them or not. We could always shoot one of the horses and skin him to look at the back of the hide—they read right that way. Trouble was, I didn't want to shoot no horse and wanted nobody else to. Moreover, there was no reason. The brands had been blotted, all right. They hadn't taken the trouble to burn over the old brand, just added to it. So a blind man could see what had been done. But supposin' he didn't want to see? To recognize the fact would incriminate several of his own men and would also mean a respectable loss of the cash money such horses would bring.

Charley McCaire was a strong-tempered man, and what happened depended on how that temper veered. Me, I meant to be ready. Horse stealing was a hanging matter anywhere west of the Mississippi and some places east of it. It was also a shooting matter, and I had an idea this Boley gent knew aplenty about how those brands were burned.

Suddenly, McCaire reined around and came back on a lope.

Orrin followed just behind Tom. When we were all together again, Charley turned to face us. "Ride off," he said. "We're through talkin'."

"Charley," Tom said, "look here, man, I—"

"Are you ridin' for the brand or agin it?" Charley's face was flushed and angry. "If you ain't with us, ride out of here."

"Charley! *Think!* You've always been an honest man, and by the lord harry, you know those brands are—"

Boley's hand dropped for his gun . . . mine was covering him. "You draw that," I said, "and when she clears leather you'll be belly up to the sky."

Nobody moved. "All right, Charley," Tom said, "I've rode for your brand for nigh onto twelve year now, but I'm quittin'. You just keep what you owe me because a man cheap enough to read those brands wrong is nobody whose money I want."

"Tom!" It was a protest.

"No."

"Go to hell, then!"

"That's your route, Charley, not mine."

Tom turned his horse and rode slowly away over the bunch grass.

My gun was still in my hand. Boley was pale around the gills. He fancied himself with a six-gun, I could see that, but he wasn't up to it.

"That's a mighty rough trail you're choosin' for yourself," I said casually. "This is a flat-out steal, McCaire, if you can bring it off."

"Don't be a fool! We outnumber you three to one!"

"You better look at your hole card, mister," I told him. "I'm already holding a gun. Now I don't know how the rest of your boys will make out, but I'll lay you five to one you an' Boley are dead."

"Take 'em, Uncle Charley," Boley said. "There's only two of 'em. That nigger won't stand. Neither will the other one."

"If you think I won't stand, suh," Judas said politely, "why don't you just step out to one side an' let just the two of us try it?"

Boley started to move, then stopped, his eyes on Judas Priest's gun. It was a Colt revolving shotgun.

"Finally got around to looking, did you? This here weapon holds four ca'tridges . . . an' if I can hit a duck on the wing I believe I can hit a man in a saddle."

Well, this Boley sort of backed off and flattened his hair down. A shotgun has that effect on a lot of folks. It seems somehow dampening to the spirits.

"Mr. McCaire," Orrin suggested, "why not give this further thought? We've no desire for trouble. As a matter of fact, this man here and those with him have already been notified of their arrest for possession of stolen property and an apparent theft of horses."

"You're no officer!"

"I made a citizen's arrest, but even so, every lawyer is an officer of the court."

Charley McCaire was simmering down a mite, but I had my doubts whether he'd changed his mind. My gun was one thing he could not sidestep. After Boley's move I had drawn without starting anything, and fast enough so that nobody had a chance to do much about it. A man could see that somebody was going to get shot, and Charley was smart enough to see he was first man up on the list.

"How do I know you ain't bluffin'? I don't know what your brother's road brand is, or even that he's fixin' to move stock."

"Unless I am mistaken about my brother, Mr. Mc-Caire, he's on the trail of this missing stock right now, and unless I am again mistaken I would say you're a lot better off with us than with him.

"Tyrel," he added, "doesn't have the patience that Tell and I have, and I think he's every bit as good with a gun as Tell, here. Back home we always figured him to be the mean one of the family."

We didn't want any shooting. The incident had happened unexpectedly, and now a wrong word could turn that meadow into a bloodbath.

The next thing we heard was a pound of hooves, and into the valley came Tyrel, riding straight up in the saddle, young and tall in a fitted buckskin jacket of the Spanish style.

Behind him were half a dozen riders, all Mexicans, sporting big sombreros, bandoliers, and six-shooters as well as rifles. I knew those vaqueros of Tyrel's and they were a salty lot. He wouldn't have a man on the place who wasn't a fighter as well as a stockman.

Believe me, they were a pretty sight to see. He always mounted his men well, and those vaqueros rode like nothing you ever saw. They were a bold, reckless lot of men, and they'd have followed Tyrel through the bottom layer of hell.

"Looks like you boys found my horses," he said. He glanced over at Charley McCaire, then at the others. Tyrel looked better than I'd ever seen him. He was six feet two in his sock feet; he must've weighed a good one-ninety, and not an ounce of it was excess weight.

"You'll find the brands altered," said Orrin.

Tyrel glanced at him. Orrin said, "This is Charley McCaire, of the Three Eights. Some of his hands got a little ambitious, but it's all straight now."

The vaqueros bunched the horses and started them toward the trail, then held up. The Tinker turned his horse and waited for Priest to come alongside. Then Tyrel turned to his men.

"We're taking our horses back," he said, "and, at the request of my brother we're making no further move, but if any of you ever see one of these men near any of my stock, shoot him."

The vaqueros sat their horses, rifles ready, while the rest of us bunched our stock and started moving. Then they rode to join us.

Glancing back, I saw McCaire jerk his hat from his head and throw it to the ground, but that was all I saw, and I was too far away to hear what he said.

Tyrel and Orrin rode point, and I guess Orrin was filling in the blank spaces on the horse stealing and then on pa. I trailed off to one side, away from the dust of the horses and riders. I needed to think, and a riding man is always better thinking off by himself. Leastways, that's the way I think best, if I think at all.

Sometimes I wonder how much thinking anybody does, and if their life hasn't shaped every decision for them before they make it. But now I had to consider pa. I had to put myself in his place.

The gold Pierre and the others were hunting seemed to be in the San Juans, and certainly, the last I heard, there was a lot of it. Also, that was a mighty bunch of mountains, some thundering deep canyons, and a lot of high, rough country no white man had ever ridden over.

Galloway and Flagan Sackett had moved some stock there near the town of Shalako and set up camp. They'd established no proper ranch yet, as they were still kind of looking around, but from all they'd said in their letters it was our kind of country.

I'd been to the San Juans before. It was in the mountains above Vallecitos where I'd found Ange and Tyrel as well as pa had been through Baker Park and the country around Durango. Pa had known that country pretty well—probably as well as anybody could know it without a good many years up there.

The way I figured it, we'd take the same route north Cap Rountree an' me had taken when we went back up the Vallecitos to stake our claims. We'd ride north from Mora, go up through the Eagle's Nest country and E-town, then to the San Luis Valley and west on the trail into the San Juans.

Suppose pa was still alive, like ma thought? Suppose he was busted up and back in a corner of the mountains he couldn't get out of? Or held by Indians? I hadn't a moment's thought that such could be true, but pa was a tough man, a hang-in-there-an'-fight sort of man, and a body would have to go all the way to salt him down.

We camped that night by a spring of cold, clear water where there was grass for the horses.

When everybody was around the fire, I took my Winchester and climbed to the rim of the mesa. There was an almighty fine view up there. The sun was gone, but she'd left gold in the sky and streaks of red, as well as a few pink puffballs of cloud.

Up there on the rimrock I sat down and let my legs hang over and looked to the west.

Tyrel had Drusilla, and Orrin had the law, at least,

and most womenfolks catered to him, but what did I
have? What would I ever have? Seemed like I just
wasn't the kind to make out with womenfolks, and I
was a lonesome man who was wishful of a home and a
woman of my own.

Folks had it down that I was a wanderin' man, but
most wanderin' men I've known only wandered because
of the home they expected to find . . . *hoped* to find, I
mean.

Looking westward the way we were to ride, I wondered if I'd find what I was hunting.

Flagan had said there were some other Sacketts out
there. No kind of kin to us that we knowed of, but
good folks by all accounts, and we'd fight shy of them
and try to make them no trouble.

Glancing back, as I stood up to go back down the
cliff trail, I glimpsed a far-off campfire, a single red
eye, winking, but with evil in it.

Somebody back yonder the way we had come, somebody trailing us, maybe.

Charley McCaire? Or Andre Baston?
Or both?

CHAPTER XII

About noontime a few days later, we rode up to San
Luis, and the first man I saw was Esteban Mendoza.
He'd married Tina, a girl Tyrel had helped out of a
bad situation some years back during the settlement
fight.

"Ah, señor! When I see you far away I say to Tina
it is you! No man sits a saddle as do you! What can I
do for you?"

"We want to get under cover, and we want a good
bait for our stock."

When he had shown us where to put our horses, he
stopped to talk while I stripped the gear from my
appaloosa. "Is it trouble, amigo?"

I warned him about the kind of people who might

be riding our trail, and then I asked him, "Esteban, you've been here awhile now. Who is the oldest man in town? I mean, somebody with a good memory that can reach back twenty years?"

"Twenty years? It is a long time. A man remembers a woman, a fight, perhaps a very good horse for twenty years, but not much else."

"This is a man—several men—who came through here headed for the San Juans and Wolf Creek Pass."

He shrugged. "It is a long time, amigo."

"One of them was my father, Esteban. He did not come back from that ride."

"I see."

Esteban started away, and I spoke after him. "These men who follow me. One of them was with my father then. You be careful, and warn your people. Start nothing, but be wary. They are hard men, Esteban, and they have killed before."

He smiled, his teeth flashing under his mustache. "We have hard men, too, amigo, but I will pass the word. They will know. It is always better to know."

We ate, but I was restless, and, good as the food was, I was uneasy. It seemed every time I came to San Luis there was trouble, not for the town or from the town, but for me. It was a pleasant little village, settled in 1851, some said.

Stepping outside I stood for a moment, enjoying the stars and the cool air. Looming on the skyline to the west was the towering bulk of Mount Blanca.

My father had been here, in this village. San Luis was a natural stop if you came from the south or the east.

The wind was cool from off the mountains and I stood there, leaning against the bars of the old corral, smelling the good smells of the barnyard, the freshly mown hay, and the horses.

Tyrel and his vaqueros came out. The men rounded up all their horses, and Tyrel said good-bye to me. They were headed back to Mora for the time being, and I told Tyrel that he would hear from us as soon as we knew anything.

Esteban came up from the town walking with an old

man—looked like a Mexican. "You must sit down, amigo," he said to me. "This man is very old, and he is much shorter than you."

There was a bench under an old tree and I sat down beside the old man. "Viejo," Esteban said, "this is the man I told you about, Tell Sackett."

"Sackett," he mumbled crossly, "of course there was a Sackett! A good man—good man. Strong—very—strong! He had been to the mountains for fur but now he was going back—for gold."

"Did he say that, viejo?"

"Of course he did not! But I do not need to know what he say. He speaks of the mountains, of Wolf Creek Pass, and I tell him not to go. He is wasting his time. Others have looked and found nothing."

"Were they here long?"

"Two, three days. They wanted horses, and Huerta sent to the mountains for them. They were impatient to be off, and of course . . . well, two of them did not want to go. I did not think Sackett wanted to go. I think he did not like these people. Neither did the other man . . . Pet-grew."

Now I just sat quiet. Petgrew? Was it a new name? Or had I heard it before and not remembered? There had been another man, but what happened to him, anyway?

Was Petgrew the name of the man Philip Baston had told us about? More than likely. I remembered finally. It was Pettigrew.

"It is cold in the mountains when the snow falls," I said. "They would not be able to last through the winter."

"They were not there after the snow fell. They came out in time. At least, three of them did. The big young man whom I did not like—he came out. So did the handsome one, who was cruel."

"And the other?"

His thoughts had wandered off. "Cold, yes it is cold. Men have lived. If they know how to live sometimes they can, but food . . . most of them starve.

"It is not only the cold. We were worried for them and thought of going out for them. Twenty years ago—

I was a young man then—scarcely sixty years I had. And until I was seventy I could ride as well as any man in the valley . . . better. Better.

"Two of them came down, and I was over near the pass then and saw them coming.

"I hid. I do not know why—I was not afraid of them, but I hid. They rode right past me. One of their horses caught my scent. Oh, he smelled me, all right! But they were stupid. They do not live with horses so they do not know.

"They rode past, but they did not stop in San Luis. They went to Fort Garland."

"You followed them?"

"No, I did not follow. Later, I heard of it. This is not a big country for people. What one does here is heard of, you know? Somebody sees. It is something to tell when we have so little to tell.

"No, I did not follow. I went up the mountain. I was curious, you see. Like the bear or the wolf I am curious.

"Only two tracks—two horses. No more. I find elk tracks. Ah! That is something! We need meat, so I trailed the elk and killed it, and when I had the meat it was late, and it was cold, and my horse, it was frighten—very frighten.

"To go down the mountain? The wind was rising. It is colder when the wind blows, and home lay far out across the plains . . . those plains can be terrible, terrible when the wind blows.

"High up the mountain there was a cave. Several times I had sheltered there. So had we all. I mean, men from this village and the Fort. We knew of the cave.

"So I went higher up the mountain in the snow, and I reached the trail up there. It was a mistake—or it was the good God speaking to me. On the trail were the tracks of *three* horses . . . three? Yes.

"Now I had to take cover and build a fire to warm me. It was very cold. I rode down the trail to the cave and I took my horse inside. I put him behind me. And then I went with my axe to cut a tree. One must be very careful to cut a tree when it is frozen. It is easy to cut a leg. I was careful.

"There was a good tree close by and some dead branches. I pull them in, and I tug on another, and I hear something.

"There was a sound, a small sound. Not the sound of a tree, not a branch breaking . . . an animal sound. I pull the branch again, and then I see it, lying over the bank . . . a branch of the tree is there, too, but it is a horse."

"A horse?"

"With a saddle. The horse try to get up. He cannot get up because he lies with his legs uphill. If his legs were downhill he could get up, I think.

"So I get his bridle. It is frozen stiff. I take the bridle and pull him over, pull his head over and hope he will keep it there. I get a rope on him, go back for my horse, and with my horse I get him up.

"When he is on his feet I look around. Where the horse was is a hollow in the snow. He must have struggled and worked himself down into the snow. He would have frozen there. But a horse, amigo? A horse with a saddle? I explain to myself that a horse with a saddle and no rider is not reasonable, you see?

"I look. Further down in the snow, I see him. A man lying there almost covered with snow. Near him are some tracks.

"It seems to me somebody has made the horse jump. He is frighten, this horse. And when he jumps he falls, and the man is thrown and hurt, you see? Then I think somebody walks down to where he lies and hits him again, then leaves him in the cold.

"It will look an accident, you see? A man thrown, frozen to death. I think they did not want to trust to shooting . . . people wonder, you know."

The old man's voice was slowing, and he was growing tired. I sat there in the darkness thinking back. A man must have returned with Baston and Swan, and for some reason they had decided to kill him. A man left unconscious in the snow at such a time would have small chance of survival, yet the human creature is amazing. Nobody knew that better than me. I had seen men survive from impossible wounds, seen them walk out of the desert or mountains. I'd had a few bad times myself.

"You saved him?"

"It was cold. It was starting to snow, and the man was not big, but heavy, very heavy, señor. I could not get him up the slope. It was steep . . . steep. Many trees and rocks.

"The man was cold—he was freeze, I think. I could not carry him up the slope."

I waited, knowing he had to tell it in his own way, in his own time, yet I could see him there at the body of the unconscious man. Up above was a cave, shelter for the horses and himself, a good place for a fire, and fuel for it. And down below there an old man standing in the falling snow.

A time or two I'd had to carry unconscious men. It was far from easy. Up a slope like that? Not many men could manage it. Probably not one in a hundred.

What to do? The wind was rising, snow was falling, and with the rising wind the cold would grow more penetrating. Maybe the man would die, anyway. Perhaps he was almost dead. Why risk his life to save a stranger who was dying, anyway?

"To climb alone would be all. I left the man, and I climbed up. It was only a little way—a hundred feet, I think, perhaps a little more, you know?

"I got my blanket roll and I slid back down. Then into the snow I dug a hole. I built high the walls of snow around us, and I gathered sticks and laid some down and built upon them a fire.

"I rolled the man upon my bed, and the night long I kept the fire going, and I was alone so I talked to him. I talked to this man. I told him he was a lot of trouble to me. I told him there was a nice warm cave above and because of him I had to sit in the cold. I told him the only decent thing to do was to live.

"It was very cold . . . *mucho frío,* señor. I shivered, swung my arms, danced in the snow, but most of the time I collected wood. There were fallen trees on that slope. And just a little way from there was a tangle of branches.

"I tried to climb up again, but it was too slippery

from other climbs, so I went into the tangle and pulled myself up from tree to tree. Then I made a fire in the cave. I must think of my horses, señor. They were good horses, mine and the hurt man's horse, and it was not their fault they were in this cold place. I built a fire up there, and then I climbed down, and my fire down below was almost gone. Again I put fuel on the coals, and it burned up.

"I looked at the man. I felt his arms and his legs. I moved them. Nothing seemed broken, so only the head was hurt. I knew the man's face."

"Who was he, viejo? Who was the man?"

"It was Pet-grew. And he did not die. He did not waste my time. He lived, señor. By morning he was a little *rojo*. His face, señor, was flushed, and his breath was better."

"You saved him, then?"

"Ah? It was the good Lord who saved him, señor. I sat by him and kept the fire warm. I kept the fire for the horses, too. Up and down, up and down . . . it was the longest night, the coldest night, and I was afraid all would die. The man, the horses, me.

"We were high up, señor. Perhaps ten thousand feet. You know what it is . . . the cold."

"And the man? Where is he?" I paused. "What became of him, viejo?"

He put a trembling hand on my sleeve. "He did not leave us. He is here."

CHAPTER XIII

Morning lay bright upon the town when we rode out of the streets of San Luis. The sky was a magnificent San Juan mountain blue, with puffs of white cloud scattered about.

Sunlight touched the snow upon the distant peaks, and as we rode there were no sounds but the beat of our horses' hooves and the creak of saddle leather.

We four rode out with Esteban, rode west to the little ranch on the Rio Grande del Norte.

It was an adobe house with projecting roof beams— a comfortable house of several spacious rooms, a long barn, corrals, and a few fruit trees.

As we rode into the yard a man limped to the door, using a cane. He wore a six-shooter rigged for a cross-draw.

He was a stocky man with a round, pleasant face, red cheeks, and a tuft of gray hair sticking up from the crown of his head. His eyes went to Esteban and he waved. *"Buenos días,* amigo!"* he said cheerfully. " 'Light an' set!"

There was a measure of caution in the glance he gave us, and I thought his eyes lingered on Orrin's face, then mine.

It was cool inside the house. "Set," he said. "I am Nativity Pettigrew, Connecticut born, Missouri bred. Who might you be?"

"I am Orrin Sackett," Orrin said, "and this here is my brother, William T. Sackett." He introduced the Tinker and Judas, then sat down.

"Mr. Pettigrew, you were with my father in the mountains?"

Pettigrew got out his pipe and loaded it with tobacco. He turned his head toward an inner door, "Juana? Bring us some coffee, will you?"

He glanced around apologetically. "Don't like to be waited on, but with this game leg I don't get around so well no more." He tamped the tobacco firmly. "So you're Sackett's boys, are you? I heard tell of you a time or two, figured soon or late we'd come to meet."

A pretty Mexican woman entered with a tray of cups and a coffeepot. "This here's Juana. We been married nigh onto nineteen year."

We all arose hurriedly, acknowledging the introduction. She smiled—a soft, pretty woman, and very shy.

"We're tryin' to find out what become of pa," I explained. "Ma's gettin' on in years, and she's wishful to know."

He smoked in silence for a moment. "It ain't as easy as you think. I took a rap on the skull up yonder and my memory gets kind of hazy. I do remember that Baston, though, and Swan. Must've been one of them hit me.

"My horse spooked. Maybe they hit him, bufned him, I don't know what. Anyway, he was always a nervous one and he just jumped right out there an' fell. Last thing I recalled, until several days later when I come to in the snow with that old Mexican—he's Juana's grandpa—a-settin' by the fire, tendin' me like.

"Good man. Saved my life, so I just figured I'd never find better folks than these, an' I settled down right here. Bought this place off kinfolk of hers."

"You had some money, then?"

Pettigrew smiled. It was a careful smile, and he looked down at his pipe, puffed a couple of times, and said, "I had a mite. They knowed nothing of it or they'd surely have taken it."

"What was the last you saw of pa?"

Pettigrew shifted a little in his hide-bottomed chair. "He took us there, right up Wolf Creek Pass to the mountain, but there was trouble making up. Your pa, he was a quiet man, minded his own affairs, but he didn't miss much. He got along fine with Pierre Bontemps. The Frenchman was a fine man, a flighty one, but strong, always ready to carry his share and more. Trouble didn't develop until we got up in the mountains along Wolf Creek.

"Bontemps had a map, but you know the wild country—unless a map's laid out with care she ain't worth the match to burn it with.

"Whoever made that map made it quick, and either he made it with no ken of how things are in the mountains or he was figuring on coming right back.

"We located some of the landmarks. One tree, all important to locating the gold, was gone. One rock wasn't shaped like it was supposed to be. Sackett found the other half of it down in a canyon where it had weathered and fallen off. Upshot of it was, we never found no gold.

"I had trouble with Baston, an' I up an' quit. I took off down the mountain. A couple of days later, Swan an' Baston caught up with me. They said they'd quit, too."

Orrin sat staring into the fire, listening. Finally he put down his cup. "And you know nothing of what happened to pa?"

"No, sir. I don't."

I didn't believe him. He was telling the truth up to a point, but he was holding back on quite a lot.

So I figured to shake him up a little. "It's ma we want to know for," I said. "She's an old woman, close on to her deathtime, an' we are wishful that she rest easy, content that pa's gone on ahead of her to blaze the trail.

"We can't let it lay, and we ain't about to. We're goin' to worry at this until we find out what happened."

"After so long a time you won't find anything," he muttered. He stared into his empty cup. "Nothing lasts much, on them mountains."

"Can't tell about that. I once found a wolf carcass in a cave that must have been there years an' years. My brother an' me, we're readers of sign. We'll find the answer.

"Fact is, I spent some time a few years ago over on the Vallecitos. I still have some claims over there."

He looked up, surprised. "Are you that Sackett? I heard of some shooting over there."

"I done my share. I came in first, and I was the last to go."

He seemed restless, and I had a feeling he wanted us to go. A couple of times I heard rustling around in the kitchen and I wondered how much Juana knew of all this.

Finally, I got up. Orrin followed suit, and Judas and the Tinker wandered over to the door. "One thing, Mr. Pettigrew," I said, "if you had trouble with Baston and Swan, you'd best keep a gun handy."

He looked up sharply. "Why's that?"

"Because they're comin' along right behind us. I don't know why they want to come back, but they do. They may figure they missed something up yonder, and they'll be asking questions around."

"What?" he got up, struggling to his feet, weaving a

little, and if ever I saw fear in a man's eyes, it was in his.

"They're coming *here?*"

"Not more than two days behind us, probably less. Yes, they are coming, and if I were you I'd get myself out of sight, and your wife, too. Better not leave anything they can get hold of."

We started back to San Luis where we scouted the town for Andre Baston and Swan, but there was nothing to be seen of them. I was coming out of the cantina, however, when I saw a man down by the corral. He turned sharp away when I glimpsed him, so I took notice. He looked an almighty lot like one of the hands who had ridden with Charley McCaire.

That set me to pondering. McCaire was a hard-as-nails man, used to riding roughshod over anything got in his way. He'd lost the game with us, but would he take it?

I wasn't worried about him tangling with Tyrel. Nobody worried about Tyrel. Tyrel wasn't the kind you expected would be taken advantage of. He was a fair man, and not a trouble-hunting man, but I never knew anybody as ready to take up trouble if it came his way.

If Charley McCaire hunted trouble with Tyrel he just had my sympathy . . . him or his boys. As for Tyrel's vaqueros, they liked him, and if he told them to they'd damp down the fires of hell.

Of course, that puncher, if it was him I saw, he might just have quit and drifted.

Still, I was going to keep my eyes open and give thought to my back trail.

We would be pulling out with daybreak, riding west into the mountains, and everyone turned in early against the riding to come.

One more time I went out to the corral to take a look around. All was quiet. The house was dark, the horses nickered a little when I came close because I was always packing little odds and ends of grub for them. This time I had a carrot for each, and I stood there by the rail listening to them crunch, when I heard a faint drum of hooves.

Now I was wearing a shootin' iron. So I just sort of faded back against the corral bars and scrunched down by one of the poles to get sight of whoever it was before they saw me.

The rider slowed down, walked the horse into the yard, hesitated, then slid down and trailed the reins. It was a woman.

I stood up and said, "Ma'am?"

She turned sharp, but stood her ground. "Who is it?"

I knew the voice, and it was Juana Pettigrew. "Tell Sackett, ma'am. I was just checking my horses."

"Here." She came at me and thrust something into my hand. "Take that, and say nothing." She looked up at me. "You are good people, you Sacketts. Tina has told me of you, and my cousin once worked for your brother at Mora. I want to help, and it is wrong for my husband not to give you this."

Then she was in the saddle once more and headed back. It was a long, hard ride she had ahead of her.

Inside the house I squatted by the light from the fire. In my hand was a large brown envelope like I'd seen them use for deeds and the like. It was fastened with a twist of string, and I opened it.

What I saw stopped me cold. It was pa's handwriting.

For a moment there I just held those papers in my hand, my heart beating heavy. Pa's handwriting . . . and pa had been dead for twenty years . . . or had he?

Juana had brought this to me, which meant that Nativity Pettigrew had it in his possession. He knew pa had a family, so why had he made no effort to get it to us?

April 20: Weather bad. Hard wind, rain turning to snow. Snow still on the mountains but Bontemps is wishful to proceed. He's got enthusazm enough for two. Don't like this. Trouble has a smell to it, and Baston's a hard man. I've had words with Swan twict over the way he treats Angus.

April 23: Clearing. Trail muddy, grass very wet. Horses about stove up. Nobody knows mountains but me. They've no idea how miserable it can be up yonder this time of year. They won't show me the map. If it's like most it just is no good.

I read on. The paper was old and rotting and some of the words were blurred.

April 26: In camp. Third day. Trail belly-deep in snow, drifts very deep. Only the fact they couldn't find anything in the snow is keeping them in camp. Situation growing touchy. Pierre straightened Andre out today. Thought there'd be. . . . Angus steady. Pettigrew talks a lot, does his work. No idea where he stands.

April 29: Moved on today. Ground soggy with snow-melt. Occasional sleet.

April 30: Showed me map. No good. Hadn't been for ma and boys I'd not be here. Chance to get enough to settle down, education, home for ma. Landmarks poorly chosen, same from several points, important tree gone.

May 4: In camp on mountain. Three days scouting, digging. Nothing. Utes scouting us. Pierre won't . . . Utes or lack of treasure. Swan sullen, Andre furious. Pettigrew quiet, secretive.

Orrin raised up from bed. "What is it?"

"Kind of a daybook. Pa's. Juana Pettigrew brought it to us. I ain't read it all yet."

"Better get some sleep. I think we're riding up to trouble. Whatever's there won't have changed by tomorrow."

"You're right." I was dead tired. We'd covered a lot of country and tomorrow there'd be more. Pa wasn't tellin' much, but a body could see how touchy things had become. Swan an' Andre sore, Pettigrew kind of bidin' his time, and Pierre still unwillin' to believe he'd lost the pot. Only maybe they hadn't. Pettigrew come out of it with enough to buy a ranch and stock it. Now that mightn't take so much, but it surely cost something.

Stretched out in bed I pondered the daybook. Pa wasn't much hand to write. He'd had some schoolin' and he'd read a lot, although his grammar was only a mite better'n mine.

Why would he write that stuff? Was there more to it than met the eye? Was he tryin' to leave us a message, feelin' he might not get back? But pa wasn't apt to think that way. He was a tough, capable man—but careful, too. Maybe the daybook was in case—just in case something went wrong.

Why had Juana brought it to me? Because it was pa's? Because it was intended for us? Or because she didn't want Pettigrew going off to the mountains again?

Now why had I thought that? Did the book have a clue to where pa was? Or where the gold might be?

Pettigrew came back with something, but Andre did not know it or he'd have robbed him. Or Swan would have.

Yet Andre may have come back with something, too. Suppose they had found some of the gold and not all of it?

CHAPTER XIV

Since reaching San Luis we had used Esteban's horses, but now we saddled our own mounts and were gone with the sun's rising. Clear and cool the morning was, and I breathed deeply of the fresh air from off the mountains.

Westward we rode, seeing the peaks loom up before us, the twin peaks of Blanca and Baldy looking from some angles like one gigantic mountain. The old Indian traditions speak of them as one—long, long ago.

We rode and we camped and rode again. At night I read to them from pa's daybook, and passed it at times to Orrin.

There had been growing animosity in the camp on the mountain.

Nat Pettigrew is a prying man, forever peering, listening, and poking about. He is able, does his share and more. He's a good man on a horse and handy with a rifle, but I do not trust him. Yet he is all for himself, and not for them.

May 20: This morning there was trouble. Swan struck Angus, knocking him down. Pierre was on his feet at once and for a moment I was sure they would come to blows. I noticed also that Andre stood to one side making no effort to stop Swan, who is his man. Andre just stood there with a little smile on his face. I believe Andre hates his brother-in-law, and I wish I was free of them, and far away.

Angus, the black slave, is a powerful man, loyal to Pierre, and a fair woodsman. I believe he'd do even better in the swamps of Louisiana than here, yet I doubt if he has long to live.

There was a gap here, looked like a couple of lost pages, then some words were smeared.

. . . suddenly there was an outburst of firing. Somebody yelled "Indians!" and we all fell into defensive positions. For awhile there was no sound, then a single shot. For some time there was no sound and when we took stock, Angus was dead—shot in the back of the head. When I talked with Pettigrew later, he admitted to having seen no Indians, nor had Pierre. Swan had seen one, Andre thought he had seen them. Andre showed a scar on the bark of a tree made by a bullet, and of course, Angus was dead.

Well, now Judas knew what happened to his brother. I looked at him in the firelight and thought I saw tears in his eyes. There seemed nothing to say to him. He stood and walked away from the fire.

"What do you think?" I asked Orrin. We were on the banks of the Rio Grande with Del Norte Peak looming to the soutwest. Orrin shook his head.

The Rio Grande headed up in those mountains in the direction we were riding, and it gave me an odd feeling to think this water I looked at was headed down toward El Paso and then Laredo, and finally to enter the Gulf below Brownsville. It was a far, far stretch.

"Orrin," I said, "I wished pa had just up and rode off. He guided them there, and he owed them nothing."

"He was in for a piece of it," said Orrin. "He wanted it for ma, and for an education for us boys."

"I wished he'd pulled out."

"You know what I think?" Orrin held up the papers and the book to me. "I think somebody in that outfit's found gold."

"You mean somebody knows where the stuff is and is holding it for himself?"

"Look at it, Tell. It needn't have been the big caches. There were supposed to be three, weren't there? All right. You know what soldiers are. Some individual soldiers may have had their own pokes stuffed with gold, and they may have hid them. I think somebody found some gold, and I think Angus was killed to take help from Pierre. I think he's next."

"Or pa," I said.

Setting late by the fire, I pondered it. Pa was up there in May. Unless it was unusually warm for the year, there'd still be snow up there where he was, and it would be almighty cold. But there couldn't have been too much snow left, or they'd have found no landmarks at all.

Of course, there were some slopes where the wind could sweep away the snow, but there was risk of a bad storm at any time.

Judas suddenly came in out of the darkness. "Suh? We are followed, suh."

"You're surely right. How far back are they?"

"They are gaining, suh. And there are more than we believed."

"More?" the Tinker said.

"They have two fires," Judas said. "I would imagine there are at least ten men, perhaps twice that many."

At daybreak our camp was an hour behind us, and we were climbing steadily. There'd been no chance to get back to pa's daybook. Me an' Orrin . . . well, it had felt almost like we were talkin' to pa, yet he was shorter of word than usual in this writin' of his. Mostly pa was a man with a dry humor, a quick man to see things, and he always had a comment. He knew most tricks a body could play, was slick with cards when he needed to be, and had seen a lot of the world, time to time.

We came up to the forks of the Rio Grande and it was the South Fork pointed the way up Wolf Creek Pass. Pa had come this way, and the fact that he was keepin' a daybook showed he had something to tell us —who else but us? Pa was a considering man, and I'd no doubt he figured somehow to get that daybook to us. Maybe he'd trusted Nativity Pettigrew to bring it to us, or mail it. If so, his gamble failed.

If he had planned to get it to us, he must have been wishful to get some particular word to us. We'd likely have to read careful so we'd miss nothing.

Orrin dropped back from the point. "Tell, is there any other way to that mountain? I mean other than right up the pass?"

"Well, I reckon." I pointed. "That there's Cattle Mountain, with Demijohn right behind it. I never followed that trail, but Cap Rountree told me of it one time."

"Let's worry them a little," Orrin suggested, so I went up to ride point. Watching carefully, I turned off and took a dim trail leading up the east side of Grouse Mountain. We followed that up a switchback trail and over the saddle on Cattle Mountain then down the trail west of the Demijohn and onto the Ribbon Mesa trail.

It was narrow, twisty, and rough. Several times we heard the warning whistles of marmots looking like balls of brown fur as they scattered into the rocks. We skirted a meadow where mountain lupine, Indian paintbrush, and heartleaf arnica added their blue, red, and gold to the scene. It was very quiet except for the murmur of the waters of the creek. We twisted, doubled, rode back over our tracks, and did everything possible to confuse our trail. The way was rocky, torn by slides. Leaving Park Creek, I cut over the pass back of Fox Mountain down Middle Creek about a mile and then took a dimmer trail that led us right over the mountain.

We rode through aspens, skirted groves of them, and then we rode across high mountain meadows, leaving as little sign as we could. If Andre Baston had a dozen men with him he probably had some mountain-riding men, but if he caught up with us I was figuring to make him earn it.

Of course, they might have taken the easy way right up Wolf Creek Pass. Indians and mountain men had used it for years, along with occasional prospectors.

More than likely the French soldiers who'd buried that gold had come down Wolf Creek.

We had come down the slope into the canyon of Silver Creek with the San Juan just ahead and below. On our west was the mountain of the treasure, and a whole lot of mountain it was, too.

Orrin pointed out a cove in the mountainside, and we skirted a tight grove of aspen and moved into a small meadow with a plunging stream alongside it. We pulled up under the trees and stepped down, and, believe me, I was tired.

We stripped the gear from our horses, and, after I'd rubbed my horse and one of the packhorses a mite, I wandered off down to the stream, hunting wood. I picked up some good dead branches, heavy stuff, and then tasted the water. It was fresh, cold, and clear. As I started to rise I heard a faint *chink* of metal. It sounded from upstream. Well, I shucked my gun and kind of eased back under the bank.

After finding the wood, I'd kind of explored along the riverbank, so camp was a good hundred yards back of me now.

Crouching near some cottonwood roots that ran down into the earth under the water, I waited, listening. The stream chuckled along over the stones, and upstream I could hear a bird singing. After that I heard only the stream.

Ahead of me, the stream took a little bend, curving around some rocks and thick brush—dogwood, willow, and the like. Searching the ground between me and that brush, I saw nothing to worry me, so I started forward, walking mighty easy to make no sound.

Reaching the little bend, I eased up on the bank to look through the brush. From behind the brush and rocks I had a clear view of fifty yards or more of the stream.

Up yonder about as far as my eyes could take me was a woman. It looked to be a girl—a chancy judgment at that distance—and she was panning gravel, handling that pan like she'd done it before, a lot of times before.

I looked up the bank as far as I could, but there was

no camp, nor was there anything like it that I could see.

Seemed to me the situation called for study, and if a body aims to study women it's better done at close range, so I came down from my perch and started around that bend. When I cleared it and had a view of the stream again, she was gone!

Yes, sir. She was vanished out of there. Now I was a puzzled man. Surely my eyes hadn't played games with me. Of course, when a man is long enough without a woman he begins to see them, or imagine them, everywhere.

I walked across that creek, which was shallow at that point, and I went upstream, stepping careful. I'd kept my gun in my hand without really thinking, except it seemed logical that where there'd be a pretty woman there'd likely be a man.

When I got up to where she'd been, sure enough there were tracks in the sand. I started to look around when a voice spoke from right behind me. I'd knowed I should have looked into that tangle right up the slope, but I hadn't done it.

"You stand where you be, mister," a girl's voice said, "and if you're wishful of savoring your supper, don't fool around. Now you stick that piece back in the leather, and you do it right quick or I'll run a lead tunnel through your brisket!"

"I'm a peaceful man, ma'am, plumb peaceful. I seen what looked like a woman up here, an'—"

Her tone was scornful. "*Looked* like a woman? Why, you two-by-twice foreigner, I'm more woman than you ever did see! Turn around, damn you, and take a good look!"

Well, I turned, and from what I seen I was in no position to argue. She was about three inches over five feet, I'd guess, and must have weighed what it needed to fill that space out proper, with maybe a mite extry here an' yonder.

"Yes, ma'am." She had a cute nose, freckles, and rusty hair, and taking all in all, the way a woman should be taken, she was pretty as a button.

She was also holding a Spencer .56 that wasn't no

way cute at all, and from the way she held it a body could see she was no stranger to its use.

She was kind of staring at me like she couldn't believe it, and, knowing my ownself, I knew it wasn't good looks she was staring at.

"Well!" she said, gesturing with the gun muzzle a mite. "You jest back up an' set on that log, yonder. And don't you go to stretching for that gun because by tomorrow mornin' your body would have drawn so many flies I'd have to find a new place to pan."

"I'm peaceful, ma'am, but if I have to be shot it couldn't be by a prettier girl."

"Don't give me that, Sackett! Sweet talk will get you no place with me!"

Sackett? Now, how in—

"Oh, don't look so surprised! Up where I come from ever'body knows the Sackett boys. How could they help it with the country overrun with them? Best thing ever happened to Tennessee was when they opened up the west and found some way to shuck some of you Sacketts."

"You're from the Cumberland?"

Her disgust was plain. "Where else? Do you conceited mountain boys think you're known everywhere? Who would know you were a Sackett but somebody from yonder? You all have those same weather-beaten, homely faces and those big hands!"

"Wasn't for your hair I'd say you was a Trelawney girl," I said, "but the only ones of them I ever met up with had black hair. Fact is, I run into one of them down on the Colorado one time, and she gave me no end of trouble."

"Served you right. Which Sackett are you, anyway?"

"William Tell. And you?"

"I'm Nell—Jack Ben's daughter."

Well, now. That made me back up for another look. The Sacketts ran long on boys, the Trelawneys on girls, but when the Trelawneys number a boy in their get, he was usually quite somebody. Ol' Jack Ben was no exception. He was saltier than that creek which runs into Coon Hollow an' meaner than a tied-up wolf.

We Sacketts carried on a fightin'-shootin' feud with

the Higgins outfit for many a year, but ol' Jack Ben, he handled his own fightin'. I also recall that he was most tender about what boys come a-courtin' his girls.

You could always tell a boy who'd been tryin' to court one of Jack Ben's girls because he walked kind of straight up an' bent back, and he never set down no-where. That was because of the rock salt ol' Jack Ben kep' in his shotgun.

"You ain't alone up here, are you?"

"S'posin' I am? I can take care of myself."

"Now, you see here, Nell Trelawney, there's some folks a-comin' along behind us that are meaner than all get-out an' no respecters of womanfolk, so—"

"You runnin' scared?" she scoffed. "First time I ever heard of a Sackett runnin' . . . unless pa was a-shootin' at him."

Darkness had kind of shut down on us. "You better get back to your camp," I said. "They'll be expectin' me back yonder."

"You mean you ain't goin' to see me home? If you're scared, I'll tell you now. Ol' Jack Ben ain't there. I am surely alone. And I ain't scared—much of the time."

CHAPTER XV

"Where's your pa?"

"He's down to Shalako. That new town over west. He's down there a-waitin' for me to come bail him out."

"He's in jail?"

"No such thing! He's—he's laid up, that's all. We come west without—well, we didn't have much to do with, an' pa figured he could mine for gold.

"Well, he tried it, and it brought on his rheumatism again and he's laid up. On'y things about him ain't ailin' is his trigger finger and his jaw.

"A man down yonder panned gold out of this stream, and he told us of it, so I done left a note to tell pa where I'd gone, an' then I hightailed it up here."

"You came all the way by yourself?"

"No, sir. I got a mule down yonder. A fast-walkin' mule and just like me he'll take nothing from nobody. I've also got a dog that's half bear."

"You're funnin'—half bear? It won't work."

"You should of told his ma that. Anyway, I reckon that ol' he-bear wasn't askin' any questions. I tell you I got a dog that's half bear."

She glanced up at me as we walked along. "You said you took up with a Trelawney girl out west. Which one was it?"

"You mean there's more than the two of you come west? How much can this country stand, all to one time? Her name was Dorinda."

"Oh-oh-oh! Maybe I got to look at you in daylight, mister. If Dorinda took up with you there must be more to you than I figured. She was a beautiful one, Dorinda was."

"Yes, ma'am, but not to be trusted. Back in the mountains we could always count on a Trelawney girl to do her best, but that one! That Dorinda usually done her worst. She nigh got me killed."

We'd come up to a shelving shore where she'd put together a lean-to under some trees. Sure enough, there was a mule, a big, rawboned no-nonsense Missouri mule that must have weighed fifteen hundred pounds and every bit of it meanness.

I heard a low growl. Mister, if that dog wasn't half bear he was half of something that was big, and he was mean and ugly. He must have weighed two hundred and fifty pounds. He had a head like a bull mastiff and teeth that would give one of them dinnysouers a scare.

"It's all right, Neb," Nell said. "He's friendly."

"If I wasn't," I said, "I'd start being. That's the biggest durned dog I ever did see."

"He's big, all right."

"What do you feed him? A calf a day?"

"He rustles his own grub. Maybe he eats people. I wouldn't know. He goes off in the woods now and again, and when he comes back he's licking his chops."

"Where'd you latch onto him?"

"He took up with me. I was huntin' elk up top and this here dog came up out of the bottoms. There's a place where the rim drops off about twelve hundred feet, and I had just killed me an elk, when this dog showed up.

"He stretched out with his head on his paws, like, and I figured him for a bear, so I slung him a chunk of meat. After that he sort of stayed with me."

"In Shalako, too? Why he'd stampede every horse in the valley!"

"He don't stampede Jacob. Jacob an' him, they get along."

Jacob, I took it, was the mule.

"Well," I got up. "Those boys yonder will think I went to get a drink and the hogs et me. I'd better start back, but you come down and see us. We'll be around for a day or two . . . and you keep an eye open for those men I spoke of. They ain't pleasant folks. Nobody you'd invite to a quiltin' or a box social, like."

By the time I got back to the fire everybody was settin' about. They'd eaten and we're drinking coffee and listening for trouble. I made no effort to be quiet, and, when I was within distance, I hailed the fire, as a gentleman should. The ungentlemanly often ended up with a bellyful of buckshot.

A man who shoots when you don't call out doesn't have too many friends, but his enemies are surely all dead.

"What took you so long?" Orrin asked.

The Tinker was looking at me kind of wise and so was Judas Priest.

"I was keepin' comp'ny," I said. "I was settin' out with a gal."

"Up here?" Orrin scoffed.

"I think he's telling the truth," the Tinker said. "He doesn't act like he'd been out among the bears."

So I explained to them about Nell Trelawney and about old Jack Ben Trelawney down at Shalako waiting for his daughter to pan out enough gold to get them out of hock.

Orrin shook his head. "That's hard work for a man," he grumbled, "and no woman should be doing it."

"Jack Ben's all crippled up," I said. "What would you have her do? Set still while they starve?"

"All the Treawney girls could cook," he suggested, "and the food isn't all that good in these mining towns."

"That needs cash money to lay out for flour and the like. You got to have a place."

"I agree with Mr. Orrin," Judas said positively. "It is no task for a woman."

We had our own problems, and that night I got out the daybook again. I gave it to Orrin to read to us.

I have been writing in secret, but it is far from easy. I think Pettigrew suspects what I am doing, but he is a secretive man and merely smiles that sly smile and says nothing.

Somebody has found gold! This morning Pierre found a small hole, dug near a tree and hastily filled in. The marks near the tree were of Pettigrew's boots.

Later, alone with Pierre, I told him the tracks were faked to implicate Pettigrew. He scoffed at me and didn't believe it. I told him they wanted to eliminate anyone who might be on his side and they would probably try to raise suspicion about me next, and if that didn't work, there would be another Indian attack. He was angry and demanded to know what I meant by that. I told him there had been no Indians, I had found no tracks. Had there been Indians, they would have returned to destroy us.

He was listening by then, and he asked who would fake such an attack and why. I told him I thought it was Andre and Swan. He was annoyed because I accused his brother-in-law. I said it seemed clear that Andre didn't mind killing and neither did he seem to mind Swan's brutality to Angus.

Pierre did not like it, but he listened. "You think gold has been found and held out?" he said. I told him that was exactly what I believed.

I took to sleeping away from the others, on a pretense of watching for Indians, and I made my bed among leaves and branches that could not be walked over without noise. Moreover I watched my back.

We read on. Pa had apparently been doing some scouting around and he had come up with a camp location—two locations, in fact. He argued with Pierre Bontemps that there had been friction within the detachment. The story was that the Utes had attacked them, killed many, and that some had died of starvation later. Only a few men were supposed to have escaped. For several reasons, the story did not make a lot of sense, for this hadn't been a patrol, but a large body of men—perhaps as many as three hundred. Pa believed there were less.

He figured there had been difficulties in the camp and they had separated. Under such primitive conditions animosities could develop, and something had obviously happened there. Pa found two camps, both with stone walls roughly put together, and he found postholes—the posts were rotted away but the holes could be cleaned out. Rough shelters—he found a button or two, and a broken knife.

Pa was shot at twice in the woods, but merely commented it must be Indians. Meanwhile he stopped telling anyone his conclusions. From bones he dug up and other signs, he decided one camp was doing a lot better than the other. The men in that part of the French military detachment were eating better, living better.

. . . must be an Indian or a mountain man in that outfit.
May 24: On the run. Wounded. We found the gold, or some of it. Andre and Swan acted at once. Luckily I'd spread my bed as usual, then being uneasy I moved back into the aspen. Had a devil of a time finding a place to stretch out, so close they were. Suddenly I awakened and heard movement, then a roar of rifles. They'd slipped up and shot into my bedding. Unable to get close, they stood back and fired. They must have poured a dozen rounds into the place where my bedding was.

I heard Andre say, "Now for Pettigrew. Move quickly, man. Tell him it's Indians and when you get close . . ." Swan asked him what to do about Pierre, and Baston said, "Leave 'im to me."

I couldn't get to both of them in time, but I ran toward Pierre, moving silently as could be.

We didn't need no pictures to tell us what was happening there atop the mountain. Baston and Swan had turned to murder as soon as night came, wanting the gold for themselves. They'd tried to kill pa first, and they believed the job was done. Only it didn't work out the way they planned. When Swan got to Nativity Pettigrew's bed, the man was gone. It wasn't until later that they discovered a horse was also gone.

Getting out of the aspen was a job, and pa had to find his way back to the camp in the darkness, expecting a shot any minute, having only a single-shot rifle and a pistol.

He was coming up on them when he heard Baston.

". . . no use reaching for that gun. I took the powder from it last evening, Pierre. Sackett is dead, and soon you will be." There was a shot, then Baston laughed, a mean laugh it was, too. "That was one leg, Pierre." Another shot. "The other leg. I never liked you, you know. I knew someday I'd do this, planned it, thought about it. I just wish I could stay and watch you die."

Swan ran up, and there was talk. I guess they'd found Pettigrew was gone. I heard swearing, and I moved in for a shot.

Eager to get a shot, and unable to see in the dark I lifted my rifle, stepped forward for a better shot, and stepped into an unexpected hole. My body crashed into a bush. My rifle went off, and bullets cut leaves near my head. Another shot was fired, and I felt the shock of a bullet. I went down, falling on my pistol. If I moved they'd hear me. I drew my knife and waited.

They did not find me, and neither was of a mind to come hunting me in the dark. I heard Baston talking to Pierre, saying, "You're dead. I will leave you here to die. You've lost blood, both knees are broken, and you'll never be found. We didn't find as much gold as I'd hoped, but we can always come back. We'll be the only ones who know where it is now."

"Pettigrew got away. He'll tell them," Pierre said.

And Andre answered, "Him? We'll catch him before he gets off the mountain. And when we do, we'll kill him."

CHAPTER XVI

When Orrin put down the daybook, too sleepy to read further, I was of no mind to take it up. Mayhap I was fearful of what I'd find, or just too tired, but the thought was with us all that Andre Baston, Hippo Swan, and whoever was riding with them were comin' up behind us.

No doubt, after shooting Pierre Bontemps and killing Angus and maybe pa, they had taken off, carrying gold with them. However, they had unfinished business. If Pettigrew got away, they had to run him down and kill him, or try. And that was what they'd done.

We were lyin' in our blankets when Orrin said, "They daren't leave pa alive. Philip Baston seemed a kindly man, but Andre fears him or fears what he can do, and Andre is his own brother and knows him better than we do."

"I'm wonderin' where Pettigrew got that daybook. Did he steal it off pa? Or did he come back and find it later?"

Tomorrow we had to go up the mountain with a lot of questions unanswered. Facing us was a showdown with Baston, and there was no low-rating the man. Some of the things we'd been reading about him in pa's daybook were clumsy, you might say, but Andre had twenty years to grow handier with his killing, and by all accounts he'd not wasted his time. All of them seemed to have low-rated Nativity Pettigrew, including Andre, and they never guessed that Pettigrew had come by some gold.

Lying there, before I dropped off to sleep, I worried some about Nell Trelawney. Of course, she had that dog . . . if it was a dog.

Anybody going around there at night would be apt to lose a leg or an arm before he knew what he was tangling with. One time I met a man told me about the mastiffs they have in Tibet. They're as big as the mastiffs we have only they have much longer hair. This Neb dog might be one of them.

Morning found nobody wishful of using language. We set around glumlike, roasting our meat over the fire and drinking coffee.

Orrin got up and took his Winchester. "Judas, stay by the camp, if you will. We can't afford to lose the stock or whatever else we've got. And Tinker, if you'll go see to Miss Trelawney we'd be pleased. Tell and I will scout around up top."

It was no easy climb. Heavy timber, with game trails here and there, and we made it up to the top. We Injuned around, looking for sign. It was there, all right, but from down those forgotten years. Marks of axes where men had chopped wood for fires long since burned up, branches cut to make a lean-to or to hang kettles from. There was evidence enough that men had lived around about at some time far gone.

We split up and worked back and forth across the top of the mountain, comparing notes now and again. We wanted to find some sign of pa, but we kind of hoped we wouldn't. When you don't see a body laid away, that person is never quite dead for you, just sort of gone away, or not around right then.

We were playing against time. Whatever we were going to find we'd have to find now, for Andre, Swan, and them would be coming up the slope. And I wondered a little about Pettigrew. He was a sly man, maybe not as crippled up as he let on.

Orrin crouched beside me under a tree. "The story has it there were three separate caches of gold," he said. "Now, even if there was only five million, it is still a lot of gold to carry, and none of them took more away than could be carried on the horses they rode.

"It is my thought, and I believe it to be yours, that some soldiers kept some gold for themselves. Perhaps they were permitted to. Perhaps they simply high-graded it, but I believe that is what Pettigrew found, and what Andre himself found.

"I think two things are at work here. They fear what

we might discover and reveal to Philip, but also they
fear we may find the gold they failed to find."

Sunlight fell through the trees, and a camp-robber
jay hopped from branch to branch above us. I looked
off through the trees, thinking of pa and what his
thoughts must have been when he had played out his
deadly hand, knowing the fall of any card might mean
death to him.

At the end there, lying wounded in the brush with
Pierre crippled and perhaps beyond help, the rest of
them riding away, what would pa have been thinking?

We had to find that place, but how, after so many
years? Had Pierre Bontemps died there?

My eyes wandered over the slope. The human eye
has a readiness for patterns. Much is not seen simply
because the mind is blind, not the eyes. The eyes
see in lines, curves, and patterns. Man himself works
in patterns simple or complex, and such things are often
evidence of man's previous presence.

Twenty years ago some evidence of the old camps
had remained, even after half a century that had fallen
between. "Orrin, there's got to be some sign of those
camps. Stone walled, they said."

"Yes, there should be something of them left." He
got up, and, skirmisher fashion, we moved off through
the scattered trees, walking on pine needles, eyes alert
for everything.

High up in the mountains you don't have to think
of rattlers. They stay down lower where it is warmer,
and they thin out mighty fast above sixty-five hundred
feet.

As we moved along under the trees the camp-robber
jay followed us, never more than twenty feet off. They
are the greatest companions in the high mountains, but
also the worst thieves. Anything left where they can get
at it is eaten or gone, and they'll do things mighty nigh
unbelievable to get at what they want.

"Tell?" Orrin pointed with his rifle. Under the trees
up ahead we could see a dug-out hole, and when we
got there we could see it was old. Somebody had dug
down four feet or so, but the edges had caved in, and

plants were growing into it. There was a patch of snow in the bottom where no sun reached.

It might be a hole dug by the folks we knew of, or it might have been dug by some other treasure hunter. There was nothing up here an animal would dig for.

We studied around but found no sign to identify anything. We went west along the slope. Right above us we could see the trees flagging as they do when the strong winds work on them, and here and there were brown tops on the green trees where the tops had stuck out of the snow and frozen.

My belly was asking questions of me before we spotted the first fort. It was lined-up rocks, tumbled this way and that, but it was clear to see that somebody had forted up here long ago. Not many yards west, we found the other camp, and right away I saw what pa meant.

Whoever built the second camp knew what he was about. He had shaped it for comfort and a good field of fire in all directions. A place had been found where boulders and stunted trees made a partial wall against the prevailing winds, which were indicated by the way the trees flagged. On mountain tops the branches are apt to be all or mostly on one side of a tree, streaming

blows.

ave arriv̲aken with this second fort,
and h̲ etter, so some of them still
ft. It was obvious that,
id, "De n the camp, each wanted
in case of Indians.

quite a battle. dians had come.
ad to be from cond circle of rocks.
ere there were tinderbox and nothing
of some quick ion.
ht have been probably sunk deep by
l, and my guess is they
aid to Orrin. Orrin. "The army ex-
he must've they would be buried to
mark only a hose little caches Baston
w probably found were
d he had me hollows of rocks or trees,

somewhere the men who hid them could grab them
quick.

"Are you thinking what I am? That Indian or
mountain man pa mentioned might have taken that
second outfit toward the west."

"Uh-huh," I said. "Two camps like this mean there
was trouble, as pa figured, and if they did go west they
could have gone south from Pagosa Springs to Santa
Fe, or even further west."

We sat silent, considering that. Our thoughts were
strangely captured by that mysterious mountain man
who was with them.

Had the military chosen him as guide? Had he come
from New Orleans with them or joined them en route?
Or could he have come upon them in the mountains?

There was a route from Shalako to Santa Fe, certainly traveled by Rivera in 1765, and by Escalante
about 1776. There could have been others before them
—perhaps a hundred or more years before them—and
any man who knew the country would know of the old
Spanish Trail.

We were on a sort of mesa above the San Juan River.
From the timber cut down and the way things looked
the French army had a permanent camp here, with
quite a few horses. Another party of Frenchmen had
come in afterwards, and they must h
departed only a few years before pa
came there.

When I mentioned that, Orrin sa
Maybe."

Off to one side we found evidence of
Old shells were lying about, and they
a later crowd. When the first bunch was
only muzzle-loaders, and there were signs
defensive positions thrown up—they mi
wiped out by the Utes.

"Pa was keepin' that daybook," I sa
"He figured somehow to get it to us, s
left his mark around here. Maybe some
Sackett would know."

"What would that be?" Orrin asked, an
there. Nonetheless, I was looking.

It had to be something that would last. We were mere boys then, so we'd not be hunting for him or coming west until years later. Yet pa was a man given to considering, and he'd talked about the western lands, had prepared us for what was to come. He had wandered the west, and he was wishful we would do the same.

We found nothing a man could tie to. There had been holes dug, some of them by folks who came later, but none of them looked ambitious. Whether all that gold was buried in one hole or three, it must have been well dug and well lined. Whoever was in command had the man power and the will, I was sure of that. Judging by what I knew of such affairs, it seemed to me they had started to break up toward the end when one crowd wanted to leave and another wanted to stay or go by another route. It takes a mighty fine discipline to hold men together when trouble is creeping up on you. Yet without discipline there is surely disaster. The best discipline comes from within a man, but you'll never get a party of men together where all have it.

This bunch had split, and most of the discipline was in the camp that had the mountain man. I don't mean one of those trappers, like pa and Kit Carson or Bridger— they came later. I mean a man who had lived in the mountains before and knew how to get along.

"Orrin," I said, "we'd better be lookin' down that trail. We're about to run out of time."

"We'll do it together," he said. "I wish Tyrel was with us."

" 'If wishes were horses, then beggars would ride,' " I quoted at him. "A body shouldn't heed what might be. He's got to do with what is.

"There's a whole lot of mountain here, and you and me packed a rifle over mountains before either of us was knee-high to a possum. Anyway, it does no good to pack up an' run. A body has to stay in there and fight. No matter how many times you get knocked down you got to keep gettin' up until the other man quits."

"Easier said," Orrin commented.

"Well, I knew of a man who was defeated by just

about everything. He failed in business back in 1831. He was defeated for the legislature in 1832, failed in business again in 1833, was elected to the legislature in 1834. His sweetheart died in 1835. He had a nervous breakdown in 1836, was defeated for speaker in 1838, defeated for land officer in 1843, defeated for Congress in 1843, elected to Congress in 1846, defeated for reelection in 1848, defeated for the Senate in 1855, defeated for vice-president in 1856, and defeated for the Senate in 1858."

"I'd of quit," Orrin said.

"No you wouldn't. I know you too well. This man didn't quit either. He was elected president in 1860."

"What?"

"Sure. His name was Abraham Lincoln."

CHAPTER XVII

Our camp was about a mile from Nell's. She had located not far from Silver Falls, and we were down creek from her just beyond the beaver ponds.

Tinker was back at camp when Orrin and me dropped down off Treasure Mountain. "She's all right," he told us. "Anybody who'd take after her with that animal about would be crazy. All the time I was there he watched every move I made and growled if I got too close to her."

"She pannin' today?"

"Some—showing some color, too. Not much, but if she can stay with it in that cold water she'll come out with a stake."

"It's better than huntin' that gold. Why, this here mountain must cover thirty square miles! There's no tellin' where they hid the stuff, and a man could work his life away and come up empty."

Orrin filled his cup. "Tell? What do you think we should do? We've found no clue to pa. If you're right and that other party went west, he might have done the same, if he got out."

"He must've lived. There's still a few pages of the daybook covered with writin'. But what he was wishful of us knowing he'd guard somehow. We've got to read carefully. I say we read what he says, and then we should work that mountain one time more. You know, pa knew the country west of here. He told us about time spent on the Dolores River."

We ate, and then we brewed some fresh coffee. Just as I'd gotten out the daybook we heard an animal coming and eased back from the firelight.

A voice called out of the darkness, "Hello, the fire! I'm coming in!"

It was Nell Trelawney astride that mule Jacob, with Neb trailing alongside. "I got lonesome," she said, "seeing your fire. I decided to come along down."

"Set down. We're about to read from pa's daybook. We've got to listen sharp for a clue."

. . . drew my knife and waited. Nobody come. After awhile I crawled out of the brush, and then I was shamed. That bullet done me no harm. It must have hit something before me. Anyway, it hit my belt and tomahawk handle, nigh cutting the belt in two, gouging the handle, and bruising my hipbone.

Nobody was around. I crawled to Pierre and he was still alive. Working in the dark I got his wounds stopped up with moss and eased him where he lay.

Two days have passed. At daybreak I set both of Pierre's legs in splints. Doubt if he will ever walk—if he lives. Made a travois with two poles, two buffalo coats. Put bottoms of coats together, ran the poles through the arms of each coat, then buttoned the coats and managed to get Pierre on it.

The horses had disappeared, whether taken or driven off I didn't know. Andre and Swan had taken all the food but the little I had in my gear, and I'd little to do with.

Taking up the ends of the two poles, I started out. It was a slow business. Pierre was hurting and the trail narrow. By nightfall I'd reached the spring near Windy Pass. I figured to hit the valley of the West Fork of the San Juan and follow the San Juan.

I am writing this beside the spring at Windy Pass. We have had a little to eat. Pierre says Andre fears Philip, but shot Pierre not only because of hate, but because he wished to inherit. "He will be fooled," Pierre said. "I left all to Philip."

We are somewhat sheltered here, but the wind is cold. It has the feel of snow from the high peaks.

"Is it not late for snow?" Judas asked.

"Not in these mountains. He's nigh the end of May, but he's ten thousand feet up. I've seen bad snow storms in the Rockies later than that."

"We get only a part," the Tinker said. "He does not say how bad it is. He has drawn that travois, with a heavy man and all they have, more than six miles in one day."

Pa was never one for carryin' on about his hurts, but he had him a badly bruised hipbone, and haulin' the travois must have been a trial for a man of his years, even one as bull-strong as he was.

Just why pa chose the western route I wasn't sure —the first of it was easier, and also Andre and Swan had gone the other way and pa might have thought they'd be lyin' in wait to see if they were followed.

Right below the spring where pa stopped with Pierre, only about two miles away, was the valley of the West Fork of the San Juan, and a lovely valley it was.

I could picture them, Pierre lyin' there suffering in his pain, pa tired as all get-out what with pullin' a load at a high altitude and his hip bothering him and all. I'd had a few badly bruised bones, once from a bullet, another time when a bronc pitched me into some rocks, and the last time when a steer flung his head around and hit me with a horn.

The fire would be flickerin' on their faces, drawn and tired as they were, and right behind them the shadows of rocks and trees.

Orrin took up reading again. He had a better voice than me, and he made a better thing of it.

Pierre is at last asleep, which gives him relief. I have gathered wood for the night and the morning fire. My hip is bothering me, and I'm afraid it will stiffen during the night. I have been thinking much of ma and the boys, wondering if ever they will see these words, if ever they will know what has become of me. They are good boys, and will grow strong and tall. I wish I could be there to see them, but tonight I feel no confidence. A growing thing is in me, not a fear of Andre or of Utes, not even a fear of death, only a fear I shall not see them again.

I was awakened by muttering from Pierre. The man was delirious, and I worried. I looked at him in the fire's red light, and he looked wildly at me and muttered about Philip. I made hot broth and managed to get some of it into him, but he talked wildly of poison, of the death of his father, of some thin red line that ran through the Baston line, and a lot that made no sense to me.

June 2: Camp on the West Fork. Pierre in bad shape. His legs in splints, but nothing more I can do. They are in frightful shape. Several times he has thanked me for staying by him.

June 3: Same place. No more than 15 miles from where we started. Ute tracks, some unshod horses, nothing fresh. I must have fires to heat water. Hot water on his legs seems to ease him somewhat. The coffee is almost gone.

June 4: Pierre is dead! Went to the river for water and returning found him dead, stabbed three times in the heart. It was no Indian, for nothing was taken, not the coffee or the sugar, nor powder or lead.

Andre or Swan? I dare have no fire now. I shall bury Pierre, gather my few things, and take to the woods.

I have just seen three of our horses grazing a little way downstream! I believe they will come to me for I always had something for them. I shall go now, and try.

That was the end of it. No more. Pa had gone to try for those horses.

"Nativity Pettigrew," I said. "He had the daybook. How did he come by it?"

"Maybe he was the one who murdered Pierre," the Tinker suggested. "Maybe when your pa went after the horses he came back, stole the book, and took off. You recall what your pa said? Pettigrew suspected him of writing things down? That daybook must have worried him."

"We've got to find that camp. That may be the last lead we get."

We sat around the fire talking it over, drinking coffee, keeping our ears in tune with the night. I was
restless, ready to move on. A lot of men had looked
for gold here and not found it, and I did not wish to
become another of them. Nor did Orrin.

In the morning we would take the route to Windy
Pass.

At first Nell would have none of it, but we argued
there was gold closer to where her pa was.

I think we all turned in figuring that tomorrow would
tell us the end of the story of pa's disappearance.

None of us wanted a fight with Andre and them.
Well, I'll have to back up on that. Fact was, I'd not
mind so much, only that it would profit nobody. I had
an itch to tangle—especially with Swan. There's something gets up in my craw when I come up against a
bully, and Hippo Swan was that.

There was nothing to be gained by fighting them,
and I was ready to ride off and leave them be. Just the
same, I felt one of the true pleasures of life would be
to plant a fist in Hippo's face. But I was prepared to
deny myself that pleasure.

Some things just don't shape up the way a man hopes
for.

Come morning we packed our gear, and we helped
Nell get straightened around, and then we headed for
Windy Pass as our first stop on the way west to
Shalako.

Looking back with regret, I saw that little mountain
valley disappear behind us. It was a place we'd stopped
at for only a few days, but I'd come to love it—the
beaver ponds, the distant sound of Silver Falls, the
cold, sparkling waters of the East Fork.

There was an easier trail down the East Fork to the
main valley, but we were wishful of scouting around
the pass, so we went up the mountain. It was just a
mite over two miles to Windy Pass.

We found signs of several old fires up yonder, but
nothing more to tell us anything about pa. He'd been
there, but so had others.

Orrin pulled up quick, just as we started out. "I
thought I heard a shot," he said.

I'd heard nothing, but Judas believed he had, too.

We rode out on the trail to the valley and turned south. To really appreciate the valley of the West Fork of the San Juan you've got to see it from north of where we were, up yonder where the Wolf Creek Pass trail takes a big swing and starts down the mountain. There's a place there that's a thousand feet above the valley floor. You can see right down the length of the valley and there isn't a prettier sight under heaven.

We turned into the trail and started along, moving at a good pace. We had Nell with us, and, like I've said, we weren't shaping up for no fight. None of us liked Andre. We figured him for a murdering so-and-so, but we weren't elected by the good Lord to put out his light . . . not so far as we knew.

I surely wasn't going to hunt him, but if he happened to come up in my sights, it would be a mighty temptation.

It was a beautiful morning, a morning to ride and feel, and we all felt the same about that. None of us were much given to talk, although Orrin could sing. He sang while we rode—"Tenting Tonight on the Old Camp-Ground," "Black, Black, Black," and "Barbry Allen." I was wishful of joining him when he sang "Brennan on the Moor," but there was no use to wake the coyotes or disturb the peace of Jacob, the mule. Only time I sing is when I am alone on a sleepy horse. There's limits to everything.

Meanwhile, we rode wary for pa's camp. A lot of time had gone by, but there was a chance we could find something.

The way we figured it now, somebody had returned to murder Pierre and pa.

Andre and Swan? Or Pettigrew?

I couldn't get Nativity Pettigrew out of my mind. He was a sly man, a murderous man possibly, but he'd had the daybook, and the only way he could have gotten that daybook would have been to follow pa and Pierre.

Pettigrew had gold on his mind, and mayhap he had found it, and was wishful of keeping it. He would have to be mighty shy of how he brought it down off that mountain. A lot of people wish to find treasure, but few of them realize how hard it is to handle after you've got it.

How do you bring a million dollars in gold down off a mountain? Mules, you say? You've got to get mules or horses, and that starts people wondering what you want them for. And you may need help, but help can be greedy, often as murderous as you.

I tell you, gold is easier found than kept.

CHAPTER XVIII

Neb scouted ahead for us, and that was a canny dog. He was big enough to be kin to a grizzly and had a nose like an Arkansas coonhound.

We rode scattered out, not talking, wary for traps because this was Indian country, but wary for those coming down behind us, too.

Pa's travois would have made an easy trail to follow, and I wondered if he, too, had feared what was behind him. When we came up to his camp we saw why he'd chosen it. That camp was well out in the open, among just a few trees and some brush, and there was a good field of fire wherever a body looked.

Of course, at first we weren't sure it was pa's camp. It was a likely spot, and there were stones blackened by fires in a clearing among the trees. We got down from our horses and, while the Tinker kept a lookout, we stood around and sized up the situation.

Nell found the grave. She had walked to the other side of the small clearing among the trees. It was there, south of the patch of woods and a small knoll. Only one grave. Above it was a cross and the name, *Pierre Bontemps*.

Pa had walked away from here when he saw the horses, and that might be any place to the south, but he saw them from here. He'd made no mention of burying Pierre, so he must have come back . . . but Pierre's killer could have buried him. And suppose pa lay in the same grave?

Neither Orrin nor me figured such would be the case, but scattered out around that little nest of trees to see what we could find. Others had been here since, and there would be nothing left unless pa had left some sign intentionally, or unless there was some item time had not destroyed.

We found nothing.

"Tell," Orrin said, "you were a mite older than any of us, and you knew pa a little better. What do you think he would have done at this point?"

"Whoever killed Pierre may have killed him," the Tinker suggested. "He may have laid by those horses waiting for your father."

Judas objected. "That is a possibility, of course. But it seems to me that whoever killed Mr. Bontemps was not one to take chances. He stabbed a wounded, helpless man three times. I believe he would prefer to wait, to catch Mr. Sackett asleep or somehow helpless."

"The way I see it, Orrin," I said, "knowin' the kind of man pa was, why he came west and all, I think, once he had the horses and no longer had to worry about Pierre, he'd go back after some of that gold."

"I think he did go back," Nell said.

"Well, maybe," I said doubtfully. "I think he *would,* but we don't know if he did."

"I know," Nell repeated. "I am sure he went back."

"Why?" Orrin asked.

"I think when he left the second time, having some gold and all, and remembering what happened to Mr. Bontemps, I think he would take another route," she said.

"These mountains offer very few roads," Judas objected, "and this is the best way, obviously."

"And the most dangerous. Best routes never meant much to a mountain-born Sackett, anyway," she insisted. "I want to tell you something.

"Just east of Silver Falls I found an old Indian trail. It heads off south along the shoulder above Quartz Creek. When I first settled in there to pan that creek I studied the country in case I had to run. I scouted that trail across the high-up mountains until I could see where it led.

"It goes right to Pagosa Springs, although there's a branch, looks like, that swings south. I've got a feeling it joins up with a trail I saw coming in from the south at Haystack Mountain."

It surely made sense. Pa was never one to set himself up for somebody, and if he now had some gold he would be doubly in danger. He'd keep off the main trails, use routes where he could find cover from which to study his back trail, and he'd head west.

If anybody was lying in wait it would be along the trail east. Folks at San Luis might have talked, and there were always bad men around who'd lie up for a man and try to gather in what he had.

Pa had wintered out west and he liked that country. If he had taken his gold that way he could come by an unexpected way and likely would avoid trouble. Still, any man packing gold was sure to be an uneasy man.

Seemed to me the only thing to do now was to cut out for Shalako, scout around there and talk to some of the Utes who might know something. Mighty few people travel through Indian country without being seen, and it was likely the Utes knew all that had taken place around Treasure Mountain—if they'd talk.

We headed west, rattling our hocks down the trail for Shalako. We knew that our cousins Flagan and Galloway had settled in that neighborhood a short time back, and we figured to meet up with them, then get our bearings. Galloway was a great hand to make friends, and chances were that he had Indian friends among them.

We Sacketts have fought Indians, camped with them, hunted with them, told stories with them, slept in their tipis and wickiups, and fought with them again. Sometimes all was friendly, depending on the tribe and how they felt at the moment. Pa had lived with Indians, too, and favored their way of life, and, of course, back there in the high-up hills of Tennessee and North Carolina, we'd had many a friend among the Cherokee, Shawnee, or Chickasaws.

They had their way of life and we had ours, and when the white man moved in he did just what the Indians had done before him. He took what land he needed. There were mighty few Indians for the size of the country, and we crowded them like they crowded others.

Life had been that way from the beginning of time, and I could see no end to it.

Over there in Europe the Celts crowded the Picts, and the Saxons crowded the Celts, and then the Normans moved in and took over the country, and it was the same story all across the world.

Five days later we rode into Animas City which they were building into quite a town. Must have been twenty or twenty-five buildings there, most of them dwellings of one sort or another.

We rode up to Schwenk and Will's saloon, which was also a store. By the look of it, this place had just been opened, but business wasn't suffering. There were half a dozen men at the bar and this was just after midday.

The Tinker and Judas took the horses down to the river for water, Nell went with them, and Orrin and me decided to listen to what was being said and try to find out what we could.

A couple of men nodded as we came in, and one of them spoke. The rest just glanced around and paid us no mind.

Nobody was talking very much. There was some talk of a railroad coming in, but it looked to me like that was nothing that was going to happen very soon.

The bartender came down our way and we both ordered rye. He glanced at us real sharp, then again. "Travelin' through?"

"Maybe."

"Pretty country," Orrin commented, "right pretty country. Much going on around?"

"Mining. Cattle. You a cattleman?"

"Lawyer," Orrin said. "But I've worked with cattle. Much ranching around here?"

"West of here, and south. Some good outfits. There's a new bunch over on the La Plata. Name of Sackett."

"Heard of them," Orrin said.

"There's other Sacketts around here. One of the first

men in this country was Seth Sackett. He came in with
the Baker outfit."

"Good folks, no doubt," I said.

"The best," said the bartender. He was a shrewd, com-
petent-looking man. "You boys could do worse than to
settle here yourselves."

"Maybe we'll ride over and see those Sacketts. The
ones over on the La Plata."

"If you go," the bartender advised, "better go friendly. They're good boys but they don't take kindly to
folks pushing them.

"They've got them a ranch over just beyond that new
town—Shalako, or some such name. They've brought
in some cattle, but from all I hear they're still sort of
camping out. Haven't started to build, yet."

We drank our rye, then ordered coffee. We could see
the Tinker had come back and was loafing near the
corral, honing the blade of that Tinker-made knife of
his. Perhaps the finest knife ever made.

"You been around here long?" Orrin asked.

"We just opened up. Nobody's been here very long,
some folks came in in '73, but the town didn't sort of
begin to settle up until '76. If you ride around much,
keep your eyes open and a gun handy. The Utes haven't
decided what to do about us yet."

One of the other men—a short, barrel-chested man
with a broad, friendly face—was looking at me. Suddenly he said, "Speaking of Sacketts, there was one
come into this country some years back. Had him a
claim up on the Vallecitos. He was hell-on-wheels with
a pistol."

"You don't say?" I said, innocently. "Well, I figure
if you leave those folks alone they'll leave you alone.

"There's something else, though," I added. "If any
of you know anybody who was around here about
twenty years back, I'd like to talk to him . . . or them."

"Ask Flagan or Galloway Sackett. They're new in
the country but they've got an old Indian working for
them who has been in this country since those mountains were holes in the ground—goes by the name of
Powder-Face."

We finished our coffee and drifted outside. It was a

warm, pleasant morning with a blue sky overhead and a scattering of white clouds here and there, a real picture-book sky, typical of that country.

"I've got an uneasy feelin'," I told Orrin.

He nodded. "Reason I wanted to get out of there. No use mixing innocent people in our troubles."

"That one man knew me, or figured he did."

We stood there looking up and down the street. Animas City wasn't much of a town, but it was growing, and it looked like there would be business enough with the mining, ranching, and all.

The Tinker strolled over and joined us. "Man just rode in," he said. "Tied his horse over yonder by the drugstore."

The Newman, Chestnut, and Stevens Drugstore was right along the street. We walked out and went down to the blacksmith shop run by the Naegelin Brothers, and we glanced across at the horse.

The brand was visible from there, and it was 888.

"Charley McCaire's brand," I said. "What do you make of that?"

Orrin shrugged. "Let's ride out."

We walked back to the Tinker and then the three of us went to where Nell and Judas Priest were setting on the bank by the river. We all mounted up and rode out. As we glanced back we saw a man come out of the drugstore and look after us.

A short time later we stopped near the Twin Buttes and waited, studying our back trail, but nobody showed so we rode on, walking our horses as it was mostly uphill, although the grade was not too steep.

The town of Shalako lay on a flat bench with a looming backdrop of the La Plata Mountains behind it. On past the town a trail went on up La Plata Canyon, following the La Plata River. There were very few buildings in the town—one of them was a saloon.

The man behind the bar was a big Swede. He sized me up as I came through the door. Orrin and the others were following me.

He grinned and came around the bar. "Tell! Tell! Sackett! Well, I'll be damned! The boys said you'd be coming up sooner or later, but this is great! Have a drink on the house!"

"We'd rather eat," I said. "We've just come in from Animas City." I drew back a chair and sat down.

"Orrin, this here is Swede Berglund, a good man anywhere you find him."

They shook hands, and then he greeted Judas, Nell, and the Tinker and went to the kitchen to stir up the grub. I wiped the sweat from my hatband and squinted out the open door. Across the street was a supply outfit —general store, miners' supplies, and whatever, and next to that was a livery stable.

When I looked across the street again two men were getting down in front of the store. They looked like they'd come a far piece, and one of them stayed beside the horses while the other went into the store.

The flank of one horse was turned toward me and I could read the brand.

Three Eights . . .

"Orrin," I said, "looks like we've got comp'ny."

CHAPTER XIX

"Could be chance," he said, glancing out the window. "I doubt if Charley McCaire's mad enough to follow us here."

"Suppose he tied up with Baston an' them?"

He shrugged. "Unlikely, but it could be."

There was no use asking for trouble. We'd had a mite of difficulty with McCaire back yonder in New Mexico, and he was truly a hard, stubborn man. Of course, this was good cattle country, with water aplenty and grass. A desert or dry-plains country rancher will ride a far piece for range country like there was here-abouts.

Berglund was putting some bowls of stew on the table, and slabs of bread made from stone-ground wheat. "Eat up, the coffee's gettin' hot."

"That peak yonder," I said, indicating a smooth-domed mountain that seemed to be covered with green growth right over the top, "what peak is that?"

"Baldy," Berglund said. "That's Parrott Peak on the other side of the canyon."

"That's La Plata Canyon?"

"Sure is. The river comes right down from the top. That's rough country up yonder, rough and beautiful."

"Heard about it," I said. "The river heads up in a big glacial basin?"

"What they call a cirque. Yeah, that's right. She picks up some other little streams on the way down. I've only been part way up. Lots of elk and deer up there, and bear, too.

"Last time I was up there I stopped to pick wild strawberries and saw a grizzly doing the same thing. I just backed off and left him alone. Ht was a good hundred yards off, but that wasn't far enough for me. It's wonderful how cramped a country can get when it's you and a grizzly in the same neighborhood.

Pa had taken off from Treasure Mountain and come down. Chances were he came this far, for he knew the La Plata country as well as that west of here. He might have stopped in the Animas Valley, but, knowing him, I doubted it.

"Orrin, tomorrow you ought to scout around for a place, something ma would like to pass her days in, where we could raise up some cattle."

"What about you?"

"I'm going to find old Powder-Face and make talk with him. If pa came into this country you can bet those Indians knew about it."

The stew was good, and, as I ate, my mind went a-wandering into those far-up hills, seeking out the way pa might have taken. The minds of men are not so different, and the mountains do not allow for much changing of direction.

If a body takes out to follow a made trail down over the hills, he'd best hold to that trail, for there are not too many ways to go. Most of the trouble a man finds in the mountains is when he tries shortcuts or leaves a known way.

Trails are usually made by game or by Indians, then

used by latecomers, but the trails are there because
somebody has found—through trial and error—the best
way to get somewhere. If you see an easier looking way
in the mountains, don't take it. You may walk two or
three miles and find yourself standing on the edge of a
cliff with no way down.

When a body sets out to find another man's trail, he
has to sort of ease his way into that man's thoughts and
try to reason out what he might have done.

Now pa was a man knew wild country. We had to
look at it two ways. He had gold or he didn't, and first
off I was going to figure it the hard way: he had him
some gold, and he had the problem of getting it out of
there.

First off, he'd head for some place he knew, and that
was here. He would have extra horses, no need to worry about that, but he would have heavy packs, and folks
can be almighty curious. And a man has to sleep.

He'd be tired, and he'd want to get out of this country and back home.

Had he been followed? The chances were he had.
Baston and Swan had left Pettigrew for dead . . . but
had they left Treasure Mountain right after that, or
weeks later? We had little information on that score
and what little we had came from Pettigrew himself.

Somebody had followed and killed Pierre Bontemps,
and most likely that same somebody had followed pa,
waiting for a chance. That somebody knew, or thought
he knew, where all the gold was, and he didn't want
anybody around to dig it up before he had a chance.

Suddenly, I got up. "Orrin, I got a sight of travelin'
to do, and I want to do it without having to watch my
back trail too much. I just think I'll walk yonder to the
store and buy something. If any of those riders are wishful of talking to me they can have at it."

"Want company?" Orrin asked.

"No, sir. I surely don't. If the two of us went they
might think we were hunting. I'll just mosey over and
give them a chance."

I strolled out and walked across the street. I opened
the door and stepped into the store.

You could find its like in almost any western town.

Bales of jeans, barrels of flour, a coffee grinder and the smell of fresh-ground coffee, prunes, dried apples, apricots, a barrel of crackers, and rows of canned goods.

Behind the counter there was a rack of rifles and shotguns; there were boots, hats, saddles, bridles, spurs, bandanas, vests, gloves, and just about all a man could want. It was my kind of store. In Saint Louis or New Orleans I could walk into a store full of things I just didn't want, but this was no city, and there wasn't a thing here a man wouldn't have use for.

Except maybe those two cowhands standing up by the counter. So I walked along up there, paying them no mind, and they turned to look.

There were things I truly needed, so I shuffled through the jeans, finding a pair long enough for a man six foot three and lean in the hips and waist. I stacked those jeans and a few things I needed whilst those gents dickered over some buying of their own. They were trying to decide about a .44 Smith and Wesson.

"But will it shoot straight?" one of them asked. "I used a Colt some, but this here gun—"

Reaching over I took it from his hand, picked up a box of shells, and thumbed some into the chambers, sayin' meanwhile, very pleasantlike, "May I settle the question for you gents? If you'll come to the door—"

One of them had started to get mad, but, by the time he was makin' up his mind, I already had two shells in the gun and he sort of decided against arguing. Nonetheless, they didn't like it. I just turned and ambled off to the door, and they traipsed after me, the storekeeper following along.

When I rode into town I'd noticed somebody had left a board standing against a rock, kind of leaning there. Maybe somebody had figured on putting up a sign and then got called away, but the board, which was about three by two, still sat there. I'd also noticed there was a knot in the board, of slightly darker color.

I hefted that Smith and Wesson in my mitt, knowing they'd always made a straight-shooting gun and knowing that I could rely on it to do what I asked. That board was a good seventy yards off and the knot was not visible.

"Now you take that board yonder? See the knothole in it?"

"I don't see no knothole," the short one said, kind of irritatedlike.

Well, I let 'er drive, right from where I held it. "Now you just go look," I said. "If that's not a hole, what is it?"

"Fact is—" I let her bang a couple more times, so fast it sounded like one shot, "you go look and you'll find three holes, yonder. If you don't find one hole atop with two on each side below it, you come back and I'll buy the drinks."

Then I turned around and went back into the store. The storekeeper went behind the counter and picked up some field glasses. "Saves walking," he said, grinning. He was a young man with a nice smile. He walked outside again.

I was shoving some shells into those empty cylinders. I do hate an empty gun. Seems almost everybody who gets shot accidentally gets it with an empty gun. When I pull the trigger on a gun it's no accident, and I never pulled one whilst foolin' around.

That storekeeper came back. "My name's Johnny Kyme," he said, "and you surely put those bullets where you said. Was there really a knot there?"

"Uh-huh. There surely was, but you'll not find it now, unless the edges."

"You must have good eyesight."

The two gents were coming back inside, growling a little and looking sour but more respectful.

"No," I said seriously, keeping a very straight face, "I shot it from memory. That's the way I do. I make a mental note of where the first shirt button above a man's belt is. Then I always know where to put the bullet."

"That's shootin'," the short man grumbled. "I figure we should buy the drinks."

"Thanks, gentlemen," I said, "but the day is young. One of these days, if we all live long enough, I'll belly up to the bar and collect that drink—and buy one."

I paid Kyme for the gun and the other things and turned to go. When I reached the door, I turned and said, "When you boys see Charley McCaire, tell him Tell Sackett sends his regards."

I went across the street for more coffee. Later on, Johnny Kyme told me what was said. That short one said, "Tell Sackett? Hell, that's the man——"

"I never saw *him* before," Kyme told them, "but he's got two cousins here that can shoot just about as good, maybe better. They just wound up a little go-around with Curly Dunn's outfit."

"Dunn? I remember them. What happened?" they asked.

Kyme said, "Oh, the few that were left dragged their tails out of here, they seemed to have the notion there were easier places to bulldoze."

When they left, Kyme said they looked mighty sober like they had aplenty to think about.

I was never much for showin' off, but if a bullet through a board can prevent a shoot-out, why not do it? I hold nothing against any man unless he comes at me, and I usually put that down to ignorance.

Now these here Three Eight hands would never have that excuse. If they came they'd know what was waiting for them.

Orrin was lounging in the door when I walked back. "Did you read them from the book?" he asked.

"Nope," I said, "I just showed 'em the pictures."

CHAPTER XX

That night, a couple of hundred yards from town, we bedded down about a dozen feet back from the La Plata, unrolling our blankets on the green grass near some cottonwoods, We were cut off from sight of the town by a wall of cottonwood, aspen, and pine trees.

We picketed our horses on the grass and settled down to sleep. Nell had gone to stay with the family who had been caring for her pa. He was feeling better now and figuring on a place of his own.

The four of us were asleep, eased to our comfort by

the rustling leaves and the water running a few yards off. I don't know what it was made me wake up, but suddenlike in the middle of the night I was wide awake.

Our fire was down to red coals glowing, and beside it sat a man.

It took me a minute to adjust my mind to it, but sure enough, there he sat, cross-legged by the fire and still as death. My fingers took hold of the butt of my gun, but he seemed peaceful enough so I just lay and watched him for a moment.

It was an Indian, and he was old. His hair hung in two braids, and even at a distance I could see it was part gray. Indians have their ways and we have ours, but a guest at my fire is always welcome to coffee, so I threw back the covers, shoved my feet into the moccasins I keep handy for nightwork or for the woods, and went over to the fire.

He didn't look up or say anything. His hands were brown and old, with large veins, and his nails were cut flat across. He wore a knife and there was a Winchester alongside of him.

Poking some sticks into the coals, I edged the coffee-pot a mite closer and got some biscuits we'd bought in the store a few hours earlier.

He had his own cup and I filled it, then filled mine. The wind guttered the fire a little and I added more fuel. The wind down that canyon could be right chill on occasion.

His eyes were old, but their gaze was sharp and level when he looked at me. "I am Tell Sackett," I said. "You are Powder-Face?"

"You look for your papa?"

The word sounded strange on his lips, and I said, "It has been twenty years. He is dead, I believe."

He tasted his coffee. "Good!" he said. "Good!"

"I want to know what happened to him, and to find where he lies, if that is possible."

"He was a good man—two times. I knew him two times. The first time we shot at him ourselves."

"Did you kill him?"

He looked up. "No! He was good man—good! The

first time—long ago—I did not know him, or him me. We shot—we missed.

"I thought he dead. I waited—long time. I went for his hair—he was gone.

"I went back—my horse was gone. Tied where my horse had been was a tomahawk and some red cloth. This is strange man—we shoot, we miss, he goes *poof!* Then my horse goes *poof.* But if he can take my horse, it is his. If I can get it back, it is mine.

"He takes it. The tomahawk is good, sharp edge. The cloth is good for squaw—maybe he needs horse.

"Seven suns. Day comes, the sun rises on my horse, tied near my head. How? I do not know. Why is horse quiet? I do not know. It is magic? Perhaps."

"My father brought him back?"

"It is so. Many suns, and one day when the people of our village are hungry, I see an elk. I stalk. I am lifting the bow and arrow ready to fly when from close under the bush where I am, another elk leaps up—all run. I miss.

"Suddenly there is a shot, the elk falls. I wait, nobody comes. I wait—nobody comes. I go to the elk. Then he stands up, this man who is your father. He lifts his hand to me, and then he turns his back and walks away. He has given us meat. It is a good thing he has done, and my people are no longer hungry.

"At night I tell them of this man, and we wonder about him. Who has sent him? What does he do here?

"His tracks are near our village. I think sometimes he watches us. We are not many braves, and there are too many young ones, too many women. I must hunt always, but the bow does not shoot far—hunting is hard.

"One morning when I leave my lodge there is a rifle there, lying upon a skin. Beside it are powder and ball. Only he could have left it. Only he could come into our village and leave without being seen. But then we see him no more."

"No more?"

"Many moons, the snows come and they go—more than two times. Three? Four? We do not know. After a long time we are in village on back side of Beaver Mountain.

"In the night the dogs bark, we see nothing. In the morning we find a haunch of elk meat hanging from a tree. Our friend is back.

"We owe him much, for when the hunting was bad the rifle he left us kept our lodges with meat. This time we do not need the meat he has left us and he knows this. He has left it to tell us he is back.

"Often we see him then, but we do not like all we see, and he faces toward us one time and makes the signs not to come near, and the sign for bad heart."

We drank our coffee slowly. The old man was tired.

"Now we have young braves. They know of the white man who gave us meat. They are like small deer—very curious. They watch. They come back to village to tell what they have seen."

The firelight played upon the seamed brown face, and the old man lifted his cup in two hands and emptied it. Once more I filled the cup. This man had known my father.

This man had watched him upon his last trail, had known how he thought, at least about some things. The white man of the mountains often fought the Indian, but there was understanding between them—rarely hatred. They fought as strong men fight, for the love of battle and because fighting is a part of the life they live.

The Indian lived a life that demanded courage, demanded strength, stamina, and the will to survive; and the white men who came first to the mountains had such qualities—or they would not have come in the first place, and they could not have lasted in the second.

Most mountain men were affiliated with one tribe or another, all had respect for Indians. Some found the only life they loved among the Indians. My father was a man of two worlds. Whether he walked among savages or among the civilized he was equally at home.

"I must know where my father died. I would like to know how he died, but to know where is enough. My mother grows old. She worries that the bones of her husband lie exposed to the wind and have been picked by coyotes. They must be buried, as is our custom."

He sat a long time. "I do not know where he died. I know he went away. He went to walk upon the mountains and he did not return. I can show you the trail he took."

"He went alone?"

"Alone—but others followed."

There was a knot lying near, and I added it to the fire, for the night was cold. Wind stirred the leaves, ruffled the flames. I gathered sticks and broke them with my hands and built more warmth for the old man, then I filled his cup with coffee and sat beside the fire again, waiting for whatever else he would say.

"A trail lies there, high upon the mountain, some call it the Ute Trail, but the trail was old before the Utes came to these mountains. I do not know where the trail leads, nor does any man, but there are harsh, cold winds and sudden, terrible storms. There are days with blue skies and tufts of cloud—but these days are few among the high peaks."

"Do you know the trail?"

"It lies there." He pointed toward the mountains. "I know where it is, not where it leads. I am an old man. I have no strength to follow such a trail, and when I was a young man, I was afraid."

"If my father went there, then I must go."

"He died there."

"We shall see." Again I added a chunk of wood to the fire. "Be warm, Old One. There is fuel. Now I shall sleep. In the morning I will take the way you show me."

"I will go with you."

"No. I shall go alone. Rest here, Old One. My cousins have given your people a place. Stay with them, guide them."

"I think soon the Indian will walk no more upon the land. When I look into the fire, I think this."

"Some will," I said, "some will not. Civilization is a trap for some men, a place of glory for others. The mountains change with years, so must the Indian change. The old way is finished, for my father as well

as for you, for the man of the wilderness whether he
be Indian or white.

"I think it will come again. All things change. But if
the Indian would live he must go the white man's way.
There are too many white men and they will not be
denied."

Powder-Face shrugged. "I know," he said simply.
"We killed them and killed them and killed them, and
still they came. It was not the horse soldiers that
whipped us, it was not the death of the buffalo, nor the
white man's cows. It was the people. It was the fam-
ilies.

"The rest we might conquer, but the people kept
coming and they built their lodges where no Indian
could live. They brought children and women, they
brought the knife that cuts the earth. They built their
lodges of trees, of sod cut from the earth, of boards, of
whatever they could find.

"We burned them out, we killed them, we drove off
their horses, and we rode away. When we came back
others were there as if grown from the ground—and
others, and others, and others.

"They were too many for us. We killed them, but
our young men died, too, and we had not enough young
men to father our children, so we must stop fighting."

"Remember this, Old One. The white man respects
success. For the poor, the weak, and the inefficient, he
has pity or contempt. Whatever the color of your skin,
whatever country you come from, he will respect you
if you do well what it is you do."

"You may be right. I am an old man, and I am con-
fused. The trail is no longer clear."

"You brought your people to my cousins. You work
for them now, so you are our people as well. You came
to them when they needed you, and you will always
have a home where they are."

The flames burned low, flickered, and went out. Red
coals remained. The chill wind stirred the leaves again.
Powder-Face sat silently, and I went to my blankets.

Nativity Pettigrew had led us to believe he had come
right down the mountain and the others after him, but
that had not happened. Somebody—maybe several of

them—had followed pa. Somebody had come back, discovered Pierre's body gone and no sign of pa, so they'd followed, found Pierre's grave, and knew pa was alive.

Pa might return to New Orleans and tell Philip what happened in the mountains. Or he might come back and get more gold. It must have been obvious from the tracks that pa's horses were carrying heavy. What they carried had to be gold.

Pa knew this country, and he knew old Powder-Face. He knew he could stay with him until he was rested and strong again, and he could hide the gold close by and Powder-Face would not disturb it. So he had come west, and he had been followed.

Lying there looking up at the clouds, I considered. I'd take my appaloosa, I'd take that buckskin pack-horse, and enough grub for two weeks, and I'd plan to stay in the mountains until I found what I was hunting or ran out of grub.

It began to spatter rain so I tugged my tarp over my head and just let her spatter. It was a good sound, that rain.

Tyrel would be coming along from New Mexico soon and he would be bringing ma. They would bring cattle and take up land at the foot of the mountains some-where. We were mountain folk, and we cottoned to the high-up hills.

There'd be Tyrel and me, Flagan and Galloway, and maybe Orrin would hang out his shingle down in Animas City or even in Shalako, although there was mighty little for a lawyer to do there. But just give folks time. You can't get two people together without soon or late they're lawin' at each other.

Far up there on the cold, gray rocks of the peaks where the last streaks of snow were melting off, up there would be strong, fierce winds blowing, weeping over the high plateaus, trimming the spruce to one level, driving the freezing rain into every crevice in the rock.

How could I find anything up there? If pa had died, what would be left of him now? Some scattered bones, his boot heels, maybe, and part of his holster and belt, chewed by wolves or other varmints.

It would be a lonely place to die, but maybe such a place as he'd want, for he was no stay-a-bed man. He'd always been up and doing, and when it came to that, what better way to go than on the trail somewhere, packing a gun and riding the high country?

The spattering rain made me think of Powder-Face. I raised up my head to look, but the old one was gone, vanished into the night and the rain as if he had never been.

For a moment he held in my thoughts, and I wondered how many times he or his kind had sat staring into the flames and feeling the rain fall and the wind blow?

Man had enemies, that was in the nature of things, but when it comes right down to it his battle to live is with that world out there, the cold, the rain, the wind— the heat, the drought, and the sun-parched pools where water had been.

Hunger, thirst, and cold—man's first enemies, and no doubt his last.

CHAPTER XXI

That appaloosa and me had reached a kind of understanding. On a chilly morning he liked to buck the frost out of his system, so whenever I put a foot in the stirrup around daybreak I knew he was going to unwind.

Naturally, I wasted no time getting into the saddle. If I put a foot in the stirrup and swung my leg over real fast, me and the saddle would come together on the rise.

Of course, I always managed to mount a little away from camp so's I wouldn't buck right through breakfast. That's the sort of thing can make a man right unpopular in any kind of outfit.

This morning that appaloosa really unwound. He was

feelin' good and it done me no harm to just sit up there
and let him have at it. Ridin' easy in the saddle all the
time can make a man downright lazy, so when they feel
like buckin', I say let 'em buck. I don't care which nor
whether.

When Ap had bucked himself into good nature and
an appetite, I took him back to the fire and lit down
from the saddle.

Judas had put together some grub and like always
when he done the cookin' it tasted mighty fine. He was
spoilin' me for my own cookin', and soon I'd be out
yonder on the trail with nobody but myself to cook.

I told them all about the visit from Powder-Face and
about my plan.

"You sure you don't want me to ride along?" Orrin
asked.

"I would prefer to ride with you, suh," Judas said.
"It might be that I could be of service."

The Tinker said nothing. He was ready to go if I
wanted him, and well he knew it and I knew it.

"It would be pleasurable," I said. "I could do with
the comp'ny and the cookin', but a man listens better
when he's alone, and he hears better."

When we'd finished breakfast, and I'd lingered as
long as I could afford over my coffee, I went to my
horses. "You ride loose, Tell," Orrin advised. "This
isn't any western outfit. They're a murderin' lot."

I stepped into the saddle. Ap had finished with buck-
ing during our little set-to of the morning, and he made
no fuss. Besides, he knew I was now in no mood for
catywampusing around.

"The way I'm riding is round about," I said, "but I
want to come into the mountains the way pa did. If I
see the country the way he saw it maybe I can catch
his frame of mind.

"By the time he started up that trail, June must have
been pretty well gone, and we know the snow was light
that year and had mostly gone off. He wouldn't find
much snow except where the shadows gathered and in
deep hollows. The trail Powder-Face speaks of might
be the one he took."

"I was talking to one of the young braves," said

Orrin. "Some call it the Ghost Trail. They say it was made by The People Who Went Before . . ."

"Well," I gathered the reins, "you know me, Orrin. I'm going to ride easy into the hills and sort of let it come to me."

When I rode down what you could call the street of Shalako, Nell was standing out before a new-built house. I drew up and took off my hat. "Howdy, ma'am," I said, "I'm off for a ride."

She looked at me, seriouslike and tender. It kind of worried me, that look did, but then I figured it was just that we'd known each other awhile, not that she was thinking gentle thoughts of me. I'd gotten used to womenfolks speaking to me and passin' by toward handsome gents who had some flash and flare to 'em. Not that I blamed 'em any. I'm just a big ol' homely man who's kind of handy with horses, guns, and cattle, which doesn't fit me very much for cuttin' didoes with the female sex.

"Now you be careful, Tell Sackett!" she said. "I wish you'd not go."

"Somewhere my pa lies dead, unburied, perhaps, and ma's growing on in her years and it frets her to think of it. I'm going to ride yonder and try to find what remains of him so ma can go her way in comfort."

Her eyes were big and serious. "It is a fine thing," she said, "but it will do your ma no good to have your own bones unburied on some fool mountain! I wish I could talk to your ma! I'd speak to her! I'd tell her what she's doing!"

"It was not her idea that we ride out and look," I said. "It was ours. But it is a small thing we can do to comfort her."

She put her hand up to me and touched me gentle on the sleeves. "Tell? Do ride careful, now, and when you're back, will you come calling?"

"I will," I said. "I'll ride by and halloo the house."

"You'll get down and come in!" she flared.

"Dast I? Seems to me I recall ol' Jack Ben was some hand with the rock salt when the boys come a-courtin' around."

She flushed. "He never shot at you, did he? You don't look like you caught much salt, the way you set that saddle! If pa'd shot you, you'd still be ridin' high in your stirrups!"

"I never came around," I said simply. "I didn't reckon there was much point in it." I blushed my ownself. "I never was much hand to court, Nell Trelawney, I never quite got the feel of it. Now if it was somethin' I could catch with a rope, I'd—"

"Oh, go along with you!" She stepped back, looking up at me, disgusted maybe. I never was much hand at readin' the faces of womenfolks, nor understandin' their ways. I go at 'em too gentlelike, I suspect. Sometimes it's better to use the rawhide manner.

Anyway, when I turned in the saddle she lifted a hand at me, and I got to thinking maybe I should fetch up to her door when my way led down the mountain again.

The trail I wanted was best found riding out of Animas City, but I figured there was no point in showin' everybody what was on my mind, so instead of taking off up Junction Creek I went up Lightner Creek and found my way by game trails over to where Ruby Gulch opens into Junction.

It was mighty pretty country, forest and mountain and a trickle of water here and there, some of them good-sized streams. I scrambled my horses up a slope onto a point of the mountain that gave me a sight of country to see over. It was open a mite, there on the point, backed up with scattered aspen and then a thick stand that climbed up the point behind.

There was a place just back of the point where a big old spruce had been torn up by the wind. Where its roots pulled free of the soil there was a kind of hollow where the grass had begun to grow. In the grass where no trees grew, I picketed the horses, stripped the gear from them, and went about putting together a mite of fire. The wood I chose was dry, and it burned with almost no smoke, and after I'd eaten I set on the point between two trees where the branches hung low and shadowed me.

For over an hour I just set there, a-listening to the

evening. There was sunlight on the mountain across from me, but it was high up, toward the crest of the ridge. There was stillness in the canyon below, and a marvelous coolness coming up.

Somewhere an owl spoke his question to the evening, and the aspen leaves hung as still as you'll ever see them, for they move most of the time.

It was a mighty fine thing setting there getting the feel of the night, a kind of stillness like you never felt anywhere else but in the far-off wilderness. There was no vanity here, nor greed, there was only a kind of quietness, and the thought came upon me that maybe this was how pa wanted to go, out on some rocky ledge with the whole world falling away before him, a gun in his hand, or a knife—the love of the world in his guts and the going out of it like an old wolf goes, teeth bared to his enemies.

I never was much to mind where my bones would lie once the good Lord had taken my soul. I had a feeling maybe I'd like to leave myself upon the mountains, my spirit free to lean against the wind.

Death never spent time in my thoughts, for where a man is there is no death, and when death is there a man is gone, or the image of him. Sometimes I think a man walks many lives like he does trails. I recall a man in a cow camp who was a-reading to us about some old battle the Greeks had fought a time long ago, and suddenly I was all asweat and my breath was coming hard, and I could feel a knife turning in my guts.

The man looked at me and lowered the book and said, "I did not know I read so well, Sackett."

"You read mighty well," I said. "It's like I was there."

"Maybe you were, Tell, maybe you were."

Well, I don't know about that, but the shadows came down the canyon and the trees lost themselves in it, crowding all together until they were like one big darkness.

And then I heard in the darkness a faint *chink* of metal on stone.

So . . . after all, I was not alone. Something, somebody was out there.

The butt of my gun felt cool in my fist. I did not draw my piece; I just sat there, listening. There was no further sound, and, softly as a cat walks, I went from there and back to my camp.

My fire was down to coals.

I brought the horses in closer, picketing one on either side of me, and then I went to sleep. Nothing, man or beast, would come near without a warning from them, and I was a light sleeper.

Once, in the night, awakened by some small sound, I lay for a time. Overhead I saw a great horned owl go sweeping down some mysterious channel of the night, piloted by I know not what lust, what urge, what hidden drive. Was it simply that, like me, he loved the forest night and liked to curve his velvety paths among the dark columns of the spruce?

I am one with these creatures of the night and of the high places. Like them I love the coolness, the nearness of the stars, the sudden outthrusts of rock that fall off into the unbelievable vastness below.

Like them, sometimes I think I have no sense of time, no knowledge of years, only the changing of seasons but not the counting of them.

And then I was asleep again and awake with the faint grayness of the morning.

Out of the blankets, I glanced at the dead coals. No fire this morning, no smell of smoke for them if they hadn't got the smell last night. Hat on first, like any good cowhand, then boots, and then the easy, practiced flip of the gun belt about my waist. Stamping to settle feet into boots, saddling up, loading the gear without sound, spreading the fire. It had left no coals, burning down to the softest of gray ashes.

A few minutes to smooth out the earth where my boots left tracks, a scuffing up of trampled grass. A good tracker would know there'd been a camp, but time would be needed to tell who was there or how many. In the saddle then, and riding between the trees to the north.

Where Heffernan Gulch came into Junction Creek there was a bend in the canyon of Junction that shielded me from downstream observation, so I took advantage to find my way across Junction and up the trail along Heffernan Gulch.

Almost at once I saw it. A deep cut in an aspen, a notch cut with an axe—not a blaze—pa never liked the glaring white of a new blaze. "If you want to follow my trail, boy," he used to tell me, "you've got to look sharp."

It was his notch, and to make it sure, another one fifty feet along, "All right, Ap," I said, "this is the trail. This is the one we've been looking for."

Ap's ears flickered around, then ahead, pricked, interested. We walked on. Occasionally I glanced back. As far as I could see there was nothing. Yet what might be sheltered under those trees?

There was one more notch on that trail, and I came near to missing it. The tree was big and old, a spruce, and it was tumbled on its side at the trail's edge. A casual glance caught the old notch there . . . and after that there were no more trees.

The trail showed no recent signs of use. Rocks had tumbled down from the face of the mountain, but there had been no big slides. The appaloosa picked his way delicately over the fallen rock, the buckskin following.

The trail grew steeper. Far above I could see the outer rim of the cirque that was Cumberland Basin. Above me loomed Snowstorm Peak, more than twelve thousand feet high, and before me and on my left was Cumberland Mountain, nearly as high. Both mountains were bare and cold, towering a thousand feet above timberline, their flanks still flecked with patches of snow or long streamers of it that lay in crevices or cracks.

Turning up the collar of my jacket, I hunched my shoulders against the cold wind. The trail was narrow, a drop of hundreds of feet if a hoof should slip. Here and there were patches of ice—dark, old ice, and old snow as well.

In places, my knee rubbed the inner wall of rocks. Further along, the mountain slanted steeply away, but here it fell sheer from the trail to a long, steep talus slope that ended finally in the tree line, a ragged rank of stiff and noble trees making a bold stand against the destruction that hung over them.

Glancing back, I caught a movement. A rider came out of the trees far below me, and then another and another.

They didn't look familiar, and neither did their horses. With my field glasses I could have recognized them, but what was the point? When they caught up, if they did, they would make themselves known, and they'd have a chance to get acquainted with me, too.

Seems to me folks waste a sight of time crossing bridges before they get to them. They clutter their minds with odds and ends that interfere with clear thinking.

Those folks were certainly following me, and it was equally certain they were none of my people. When they caught up there'd likely be trouble, but I wasn't going out hunting it. I was looking for signs of pa.

Far and away on my right lay a vast and tumbled mass of distant peaks and forest, bare rock shoved up here and there, high mountain parks and meadows . . . magnificent country. Overhead, the sky was impossibly blue and dotted with those white fluffs of cloud that seemed always to float over the La Platas and the San Juans. Trouble coming or not, this was great country, a man's country.

The trail took a turn and I lost sight of them below. Alongside the trail there was a beautiful little patch of blue, like a chunk of the sky had floated down to rest on that frost-shattered rock and gravel beside the trail— it was some alpine forget-me-not. Down the steep slope where a fallen man or horse would roll and tumble for seven or eight hundred feet, I could see the bright gold of avalanche lilies here and there.

The last few yards was a scramble, but Ap was a mountain horse and the buckskin seemed content to follow any place Ap would go.

When we topped out on the rim there was a view you wouldn't believe. Down below us was a huge basin, one side opening and spilling down into La Plata Canyon. There was another vast glacial gouge on my left, and ahead of me I could see the thread of that high, ancient trail winding its way across the country, a thin thread through the green of the high grass that was flecked with wild flowers of every description.

All around were vast and tumbled mountains. I was twelve thousand feet above sea level. Far off to the north I could see the great shaft of the Lizard Head and get a glimpse of Engineer Mountain, and off to the east were the Needles, White Dome, Storm King, and what might be the Rio Grande Pyramid, near which the Rio Grande rises. It was the kind of view that leaves a man with a feeling of magnificence, but there just ain't words to cover it.

Old Ap, he seemed happy on that high place, too, but he snorted a little when I started him down the thread of trail that led through the gravel and the frost-shattered rocks on the inside of the cirque.

It was like going down the inside of a volcanic crater, only there was a meadow at the bottom and no fires.

The man lying under the spruce had been there since shortly after daylight. He had a Sharps rifle, one of the best long-range weapons there is, and he had a natural rest across the top of a fallen tree. His view of the trail down the inside of the rim was clear and perfect, and when he saw Tell Sackett top the rim he was pleased. This was going to be the easiest hundred dollars he had ever earned—and it surely beat punching cows.

He was a dead shot, a painstaking man with a natural affinity for weapons and a particular ease with rifles. He let Sackett come on, shortening the distance for him.

He picked his spot, a place where the steepness of the trail seemed to level off for a few feet. When Sackett reached there, he would take him. The range was roughly four hundred yards—possibly a bit over. He had killed elk at that distance, and kills had been scored with a Sharps at upwards of a thousand yards.

He sighted, waited a little, then sighted again. About twenty yards now . . . he settled himself into the dirt, firmed his position. Sackett was a salty customer, it was said. Well, soon he'd be a salted customer.

He looked again, sighted on a spot below the shoulder and in a mite toward the chest, took a long breath, eased it out, and squeezed off his shot.

The best laid plans of mice and men often seem to be the toys of fate. The marksman had figured on everything that could be figured. His distance, the timing, the fact that the rider was at least a hundred and fifty feet higher than himself. He was a good shot and he had thought of it all.

He had the rider dead in his sights, and a moment after the squeeze of the trigger William Tell Sackett should have been bloody and dead on the trail.

The trouble was in the trail itself.

At some time in the not too distant past, nature had taken a hand in the game, and in a playful moment had trickled a small avalanche off the rim, down the slope, and across the trail. In so doing it left a gouge in the trail that was about a foot deep.

As the marksman squeezed off his shot, the appaloosa stepped down into that gully. The drop—as well as the lurch in the saddle that followed—was just enough. The bullet intended for Tell's chest nicked the top of his ear.

The sting on my ear, the flash of the rifle, and the boom that followed seemed to come all at once, and whatever else pa taught us boys he taught us not to set up there and make a target of yourself.

Now it was a good hundred and fifty yards to the foot of the trail and every yard of it was bare slope where I'd stand out like a whiskey nose at a teetotalers' picnic. So I just never gave it a thought, there wasn't time for it. I just flung myself out of that saddle, latching onto my Winchester as I kicked loose and let go. I hit that slope on my shoulder, like I'd planned, rolled over and over, and came up at the base of the slope with my rifle still in my hands and a mad coming up in me.

Nobody needed to tell me that anybody shooting at me now had been posted and waiting for me. This was some sure-thing killer out scalp hunting, and I have a kind of feeling against being shot at by strangers. Least a man can do is introduce himself.

When I reached the bottom of that slope I had a second boom ringing in my ears, but that shot—it sounded like a Sharps buffalo gun so he must have reloaded fast—had missed complete. Nonetheless the thing to do at such a time is be someplace else, so I rolled over in the grass, hit a low spot, and scrambled on knees and elbows, rifle across my forearms, to put some distance from where I fell.

Chances were nine out of ten he figured he'd got me with the first shot, because I fell right then. Chances also were he'd wait a bit and if I didn't get up he'd come scouting for the body, and I meant to be damned sure he found one . . . his.

Ap had stopped only a moment. That was a right sensible horse and he knew he had no business up there on that bare slope, so he trotted along to the bottom. The buckskin stayed right with him, the lead rope still snubbed to the saddle horn. I was going to need those horses so I kept an eye on them. Pretty soon they began to feed on the meadow.

When I'd scrambled fifty yards or so, I was behind a kind of low dome, maybe some dirt pushed up by the last small glacier when it slid off the walls and pushed along the bottom of the cirque.

My ear was bleeding and it stung like crazy, and that kind of riled me, too. That man over yonder sure had a lot to answer for.

Careful to keep my rifle down so the sun wouldn't gleam on it, I edged along that earth dome until I was on the far shoulder of it. Then I chanced a look toward those spruce trees where the shot had come from.

Nothing.

Minutes passed. About that time a thought occurred to me that had me sweating.

Those folks coming up the trail back of the mountain would be topping out on the crest and looking down into that basin. Now while that sport over yonder with the Sharps couldn't see me—at least I hoped he couldn't —I'd be wide open and in the clear for those people when they topped out on the rim.

They'd have me from both sides and I'd be a dead coon.

I've been shot at now and again, and I've taken some lead here and there, but I never cared for it much. To tell you the truth, I'd as leave let it lay. There's some-

thing mighty disconcerting about a bullet in the brisket
. . . lead sets heavy on the stomach.

The trouble was I'd about run out of places to go.
From here on, I was in the open unless I could squeeze
right into the ground. Nowhere could I see more than
two or three inches of cover, and I was going to want
more—a whole lot more.

One thing I did know. If those people topped out on
that rise and raised a gun at me, they were going to find
it was an uncomfortable place to be. Because I was
going to start shooting, and their horses would come
down off that rim one way or the other, probably running and buck-jumping.

Of a sudden I heard a faint stir, and I turned very
carefully.

A man, rifle held in his hands ready for use, was
standing just in front of the spruce trees. He was standing stock-still and he was listening.

I eased my rifle forward and waited. The man stood
there, took a couple of steps forward, and stopped
again. From where I'd fallen when he fired he would
be merged against that spruce background and not
easily seen; from where I now lay he was outlined stark
and clear. He took another step forward, and then one
of the riders topping the ridge evidently got a glimpse
of me. He up with his rifle and let drive, and I shot at
the man by the spruce trees.

I left the ground in a diving run. I had no hopes of
scoring a good hit, but the bullet turned him. As I had
run to his right, which meant he had to swing toward
the hard side, he missed his shot at me. I went into
some hummocks of grass and rubble, rolled over three
times, and took another diving run into the woods.

Turning, I shot three times at the bunch on the ridge
as fast as I could work the lever on the Winchester. I
was shooting at a target seven or eight hundred feet
higher and some distance off, but the bullets lit among
them.

Like I figured, it blew things all to bloody hell. One
of those horses jumped right straight out ahead of him,
hit that slope on all fours, went to his knees, throwing

his rider, and, still sliding, scrambled up and made it to the bottom.

Another of the horses came down the slope on that narrow path hell-bent for election with the rider hanging on with both hands. The horse hit the bottom of the trail and stopped short, and the rider went right on over his head. He hit hard, got up, and fell over.

The other two who had been up there disappeared down the other side. I kept on moving. Somewhere in this same patch of woods was that killer who had come close to notching my skull a few minutes back.

If I'd put a bullet in him, I'd be lucky, but I might just have burned him or his rifle or hit near him. Any one of those things can make a man jump.

I lit out at a run along the slope, keeping into the trees. Mostly I went downhill because that was the easiest way to go. Then I slowed down and worked my way along the slope to get to where Ap was feeding.

There were dips and hollows in the land, brush and trees here and there, but mostly just grass and flowers. The rim of the cirque was just over yonder, so I went that way, doing the Injun in the grass, snaking along when necessary, running when I could.

At that altitude, even if you're used to it as I was, you just don't do much running. Finally I hunkered down between three thick-boled old spruce and waited, catching my breath and trying to see where they were located.

My horses were grazing about a hundred yards off, and one of theirs, his saddle under his belly, stood spraddle-legged about that same distance away but closer to where they must be.

Having a moment to spare, I fed some shells into my rifle and held my place. At least two of them had reached the bottom, and one was in no shape for action, judging by the tumble taken. One of them was out in front of me somewhere and so was the one who first shot at me.

Time dragged by slowly. Shadows began to gather in the basin. On the rim there was golden sunlight, and there was a pinkish tinge to the clouds. Out over the basin, somebody called . . . it sounded like a woman, but that couldn't be.

Looking toward my horses, I decided to try for them. I went forward, keeping to the deepest grass and wild flowers, some of which were almost waist-high.

No telling who they were out there. Andre Baston and Hippo Swan? Probably. But they had started one bunch of killers after me a good while back, and they'd surely not hesitate to try again. Killing was something you could buy cheap, these days. The chances of being charged with a killing out here were slight. Many men went west, many never came back, and few questions were asked.

It took me some stretch of time before I reached my horses, even though they weren't far off. I moved along, keeping out of sight as best I could, and heard nothing. And then, just as dark was coming on the rim up yonder, I saw a rider top out there, hold fast for a minute, and start down the trail. All he could see from up there was a great black bowl of darkness.

As I edged closer, old Ap pricked his ears and took a step toward me, curious as to why I was down there on the ground. "Easy, boy!" I whispered. "Easy, now!"

He stood fast and my hand went out to gather up the reins. I drew the horse nearer to me, then, carefully, I got to my feet.

Suddenly, at my elbow, a voice spoke—a woman's voice. The shock of it sent a chill right up my spine.

"I believe I have been hurt. Can you help me?"

CHAPTER XXII

It was Fanny Baston.

She had a voice that was one in ten thousand—low, soft, inviting. Even in the darkness I could see there was blood on her face, her blouse and coat were torn, and she was favoring one leg.

"Your friends are close by." I wanted no part of her, just none at all. She was hurt, all right, but she had a

brother and an uncle within call, and mayhap others as
well.

"I think I am . . ." she just let go everything and
slumped to the ground, passed out.

I swore. Yessir, I swore. The last thing I needed right
now was to be saddled with a hurt woman, especially
this one. She hadn't seemed to know me. Maybe that
rap on the skull had done it, but there wasn't much a
body could do.

If I called for them, I'd get shot. If I left her there,
she might die. I'd no idea how bad off she was, and I
couldn't see any way but to take her along. So I picked
her up and put her in the saddle. Holding her with one
hand I started forward. I hadn't gone that way more
than a few minutes when Ap stopped. I tried to urge
him on, but he wouldn't budge a step. Leaving Fanny
Baston slumped over the saddle horn, I went forward
and almost stepped off of the world.

My foot went off the edge, and it was lucky I had
hold of the bridle. Pulling back, I knocked a small rock
off into space, and it fell what seemed like a long time.
I backed up and turned the horse, and we worked back
into the scattered trees and into the grass.

What I needed now was a hideout. Wandering
around in the dark at the edge of a cliff was no way to
find one, yet find one I did. It was fool's luck, nothing
else.

I came to another place where the horse stopped, but
that time I could see trees ahead of me. I dropped a
rock and it fell only a few feet and lit soft.

I worked along the edge until I found a place that
sort of slanted off and I went down. I was on a lower
level, maybe six or eight feet lower than where I'd been,
and there was thick grass underfoot.

I had tied Fanny's hands to the pommel, and now I
led the horses down and along under the trees. When I
got behind a small shoulder of that ledge, I pulled up,
knelt close to the ground, and took the chance to strike
a match.

Some tall spruce, boles eight to ten inches through,
were close around me. I was on level, grassy ground.

I untied Fanny's hands and lifted her down. She was

unconscious, or seemed to be. If she was shamming, she was doing an almighty good job of it. I put her on the grass, stripped the gear from my horses, and led them over on the grass and picketed them.

Coming back to the trees, I stood there for a moment, getting the feel of the place. All around me was darkness, overhead a starlit sky except where the limbs of spruce intervened.

We seemed to be in a sort of pocket. One edge of it, I was quite sure, was the lip of that drop-off over which I'd almost stepped—the outer edge of the mountain itself.

Down here, and under the spruce, there seemed a good chance a fire would not be seen. In the dark I surely could do nothing for that girl, and I was hungry and wanting coffee.

Breaking a few of the dried suckers from the trees and gathering wood by the feel, I put together enough for a fire, then lit a small blaze.

Fanny Baston was out cold, all right, and she was pale as anybody I'd seen who was also alive. She'd had a nasty blow on the skull and her head was cut to the bone. One arm was scraped, taking a lot of the hide off. Her leg wasn't broken, but there was a swelling and a bruised bone. I heated water, started coffee, and bathed some of the blood off her face and head. I also bathed the arm a little, getting some of the grass and gravel out of the skinned place.

I took the thong off my six-shooter. If I needed a gun I was going to need it fast. My Winchester I kept to hand, but across the fire from that woman.

By the time I'd made coffee her breathing was less ragged and she was settling down into what seemed to be a natural sleep. She was a beautiful woman, no denying it, but here I was, so weary I scarce could stand, and I dasn't sleep for fear she'd wake up in the middle of the night and put a blade into me.

And she had one. She had it strapped to her leg under her dress, a neat little knife, scarcely wider than her little finger but two-edged as well as pointed. I'd come onto it whilst I was checking that bad leg, but I left it right where it was.

After a bit I walked off into the dark and went back up on the level. There was no sign of that place from above, and the little fire I had was well hidden. I listened for a spell, then strolled back. Fanny Baston had not moved. At least not so's I could see.

Taking my blankets I moved back among those trees. Three spruces grew together, their trunks starting almost from the same spot. I settled down amongst them with my pistol hitched around between my legs and my Winchester handy. Wrapped in a blanket, I settled down for the night.

The trees formed a V and I put a couple of small branches across the wide part of it. To reach me they'd have to step one foot there, and I had a notion I'd hear them first. And there was always the horses to warn me of folks a-coming.

There for a time I slept, dozed, slept again, and dozed. Then I was awake for a spell. Easing out of my place I added a few small sticks to the fire, checked Fanny, covering her better with the blanket, then went back to my corner.

It was not yet daybreak when I finally awakened, and I sat there for a bit, thinking about pa and about this place and wondering what had become of him.

Wherever he'd come to the end could not be far from here unless he taken that ghost trail clean out of the country. Knowing pa, he might have done just that. I was wishing I had ol' Powder-Face with me. That was a canny Injun, and he'd be a help to a man in sorting out a twenty-year-old trail.

When the sky was gray I eased out of my corner and stretched to get the stiffness out of me. I was still tired, but I knew that this day I had it to do.

First off I strolled over to the rim. There was a drop of around a thousand feet, and, at the point where I'd almost stepped off, a sheer drop. Far off I could see a red cliff showing above the green, and still further the endless mountains rolling away like the waves of the sea to the horizon.

There was no easy way into that vast hollow, but on a point some distance off there was the thin line of a game trail, probably made by elk. It might lead into the basin.

I started back to camp.

Nobody needed to tell me the showdown was here. It was now; it was today.

Andre Baston had followed me from New Orleans, and with him Hippo Swan. They knew what happened here twenty years ago. That Fanny Baston had come with them was a measure of their desperation.

They'd lived mighty easy most of their days. They'd built themselves a style of life they preferred, and then they discovered that money did not last forever. Ahead of them was loss of face and poverty, and all that would go with it, and they had no courage to face what many face with dignity their life long.

They had staked everything on what would happen today. Not only to prevent the discovery of what had gone before, but if possible to find the treasure—or a part of it—for themselves.

When daylight came I could see that I was on a sort of ledge that sat like a step below the rim. It was covered with grass and scattered with trees and it seemed to curve on around until it lined out along a great bare-backed ridge.

The ledge varied in width, maybe a hundred feet at its widest point, narrowing down here and there to no more than a third of that. It was a place that no one would suspect until they were right on it, and I couldn't have found anything better.

From anywhere on that ledge a body could see most of it, and I could see no movement yonder where Fanny Baston was lying. I went to my horses and moved them further along. This was good grass and they were having a time of it; and they deserved it.

Nevertheless, being a man who placed no trust in any future I had not shaped myself, I packed my saddle yonder and slapped it on the appaloosa. Then I put together most of my gear and took it down behind a shoulder of rock near the buckskin.

Right above the ledge was a high, rocky knoll that overlooked everything around. From the ledge I could crawl out and climb that knoll and have a good view of the whole basin.

First I walked back to camp. Fanny Baston was sitting up, her arms around her knees. She looked up at me, her eyes blank.

"Where is this place?" she asked.

"On top of a mountain," I said. I did not know what to think of her, and I was careful. My right hand held my rifle by the action, thumb on the hammer in case of unexpected company. "You had a fall. Your horse jumped off the trail."

She looked at me. "Are you taking care of me? I mean . . . why are we here?"

She seemed genuinely puzzled, but I was of no mind to play games. I knew the showdown was close to hand. "You followed me to kill me," I said. "You and your uncle and them."

"Why should we want to kill you?" She looked mystified. "I can't imagine wanting to kill you, or hurt you—you're—you're nice."

She said it in a little girl's voice. "And you're so tall, so strong looking." She got up. "Are you strong? Could you hold me?"

She took a step toward me. Her dress was torn and her shoulder was bare above that scraped-up arm.

"Your brother and your uncle are right over yonder," I said, "and if you start walking that way, they'll find you."

"But—but I don't *want* to go! I want to stay with you."

"You must have taken more of a rap on the skull than I figured," I told her. "You're a right fine lookin' figure of a woman, but I wouldn't touch you with a hayfork, ma'am. I don't think you've got an honest bone in you."

She smiled. "I *do* like you!"

She came toward me, moving in close. "Tell, please! Let's forget all this! Let's take the horses and go back down the way we came! We could keep right on—to California! Anywhere!"

"Yes, ma'am. We could, but—"

Suddenly, she jumped at me, grabbing at my rifle with

both hands. She latched on to it and then she grabbed my wrist. *"Now,* Paul! *Now!"*

Scared, I threw her off me, sending her tumbling on the grass. She cried out as she hit, and I lost balance and went to one knee.

Paul was standing there, a rifle in his hands, and, even as I looked, its muzzle stabbed flame.

CHAPTER XXIII

Paul was no such killer as his uncle. He shot too quickly and at a moving target, and his bullet missed. Mine did not.

Yet it was an almost miss. The bullet I had intended for his body was high. It struck the action of the rifle, ripping into his hand, cutting a furrow along his cheek, and taking the lobe from his ear.

He screamed, dropped the rifle, and ran.

Fanny, crying hoarsely with anger, scrambled to her feet and ran for the rifle. I struck her aside, knocking her into the grass once more. I picked up the rifle and threw it.

It cleared the edge and fell, disappearing from sight.

Someone shouted, "They've found him! Come on!"

I turned and ran swiftly back toward my horses, keeping trees between me and them. I heard a shot, and a bullet scattered twigs and bark over my head, so I swung behind a tree, gasping for breath, but ready to shoot.

There was no target.

Then I heard Fanny shouting, her voice hoarse and angry. "Paul had him! He shot right at him and missed! And then he ran like a rabbit!"

It was easy to cast blame. Chances were Paul had never faced gunfire before. Like a lot of others he was ready to hurt or kill, but not to be hurt or killed.

Many men avoid battle not from cowardice but from fear of cowardice, fear that when the moment of truth comes they will not have the courage to face up to it.

Paul had no such nerve, and he had been hurt—perhaps not badly, and certainly not fatally, but he had seen his own blood flowing, a profound shock to some.

"It is no problem," I heard Andre's voice, calm and easy. "No problem. I know the place where he is, and there's no way out. It worked before and it will again."

Before?

I looked around me.

Here? Had this been where pa died? I looked toward the corner where the horses were. There?

I had seen no bones, no grave. Wild animals might have scattered the bones, or the body might have been thrown over the edge into the hollow below.

Here . . . had pa come to an end here? And was I to follow him?

The situation was different, I told myself. I had a good Winchester, plenty of food, ammunition . . . I could stand a siege. Unless there was something else, some unknown factor.

Some time back Judas had said that Andre Baston had ten men with him. It might be an exaggeration, but there were several. I could hear their voices.

After a moment, seeing all clear, I retreated to where the horses were. Here the cul-de-sac narrowed down, and the drop into the basin below was steep. Even had a man been able to get down there, until he could reach the trees, he would be wide open for a shot from the rim. And Andre wasn't likely to miss, as Paul had.

It looked like there might be a narrow way along the rim, a way that might be used by man or horse, but it showed no tracks, no trail, no sign of use. There was also a good chance that a rifleman would be waiting at the other end, with a certain target. There'd be no chance of missing if the target was approaching over a way not three feet wide.

Some rocks had been heaped up here, one slab on another, and some had fallen from a higher barricade. Now there was a fallen tree, the needles still clinging to the dead branches.

When I reached the horses I broke open a box of cartridges and filled my coat pockets. My Winchester

'73 was fully loaded, and I was ready as a man could be.

Right over beyond that bare knoll that towered above me was the basin, and from the lower side of the basin a trail went down La Plata Canyon to Shalako.

At Shalako were at least three Sacketts and some friends, but that was six or seven miles away, maybe further, and they might as well be in China for all the good they'd do.

What happened here was up to me. And only me.

I just had a thought that worried me. It passed through my mind while I was considering other things. Something was suddenly nagging me . . . what could it have been?

There was some factor in my setup here . . .

I had a good field of fire down the ledge from where I'd chosen my hiding place. There were a few dips and hollows, some fallen logs, some of them almost rotted through.

Getting the horses into as safe a spot as could be, I settled down and gave study to the situation. Over my shoulder I could see the almost bare flank of that ridge where the ghost trail led. Now if I could get over there. . . .

Nobody was coming. Evidently they were sure they had me and would let me worry a mite. I smelled smoke . . . they were fixing some breakfast.

Well, why not me?

I gathered some sticks and put together a bit of a blaze and set some coffee to boiling. Then I got out my skillet and fried up some bacon. Meanwhile I kept an eye open for those gents who were hunting me.

If this was where they had cornered pa, where were his bones? And what became of his outfit? And the gold?

Pa was a canny man, and he'd not be wishful of them profiting by his death. If this was where it happened, then he would have made some show of hiding things.

Yet, how had it happened? True, pa only had a muzzle-loader, and, fast as he was, he'd not be able to fight off a bunch of them for long. But he had a pistol —or should have had.

Thing that disturbed me was the fact that Baston and them were so sure they had me. Now if I could just see what they were about . . .

Suddenly a cold chill went through me, like they say happens when somebody steps on your grave.

All of a sudden I knew why they were so sure of themselves.

They had a man atop that knoll who could shoot into this place where I was.

He was probably up there now, and, when the attack began and my attention was directed down along the ledge, he'd shoot me from the top of that hill. Actually, it was a peak, standing higher than anything close by. Looking up at it, I could see where a man up there, if willing to expose himself a little, could fire at almost every corner of this ledge—*almost* every corner.

Well, cross that bridge when it came. Now for the bacon. I ate it there, liking the smell of it and the smell of the fire. What would I miss most, I wondered, if I should be killed here? The sight of those clouds gathering over the mountains yonder? The smell of wood-smoke and coffee and bacon? The feel of a good horse under me? Or the sunlight through the aspen leaves?

I hadn't a lot to remember, I guess. I'd been to none of the great places, nor walked among people of fame. I'd never eaten very fancy, nor been to many drama-shows. I'd set over many a campfire and slept out under the stars so much I knew all their shapes and formations from looking up at them time after time.

There'd been some good horses here and there, and some long trails and wide deserts I'd traveled. I had those memories, and I guess they stacked up to quite a lot when a fellow thought of it. But pa was away head of me when he settled down here to make his stand. He had a wife back home, and some boys growing, boys to carry on his name and carry on his living for him. I hadn't a son nor a daughter. If I went out now there'd be nobody to mourn me. My brothers, yes. But a man needs a woman to cry for him when he goes out.

Still, I'd want to be the last to go. I'd want to see her safely to bed before I cashed in my checks. Maybe it is easier for a man to be alone than a woman. I wouldn't know much about such things.

They are gettin' busy over yonder. Voices are closer. I reckon the fussin' and the feudin' are shapin' up to start. I reckon this is how some of those old Trojans felt when they put on their armor for the last fight, when the Greeks were closing in and they knew they weren't going to make it.

But I am going to make it. No man should go down the long way without leaving something behind him, and all I've got to leave will disappear when the dust settles.

A man can carve from stone, he can write fine words, or he can do something to hold himself in the hearts of people. I hadn't done any of those things, not yet.

Maybe I never would.

The wind was dying. Leaves hanging still. There was the coolness of the mountains around me. This here place must be close onto twelve thousand feet up. A shade less, because there were trees around me. But the trees stopped not fifty yards off, and even here there weren't very many.

Looked like something moved atop that knoll. I'd like to burn him a mite, like to singe his scalp so's he'll know it ain't all going to be fun.

They were comin' now. Some movement down the ledge. I ate the last strip of bacon and refilled my cup with coffee.

A bullet nudged at the rock over my head, spilling fragments into my coffee. I swore. Now they shouldn't ought to have done that. A body can take just so much, and I set store by a good cup of coffee.

If I stayed back close to the rocks nobody was going to get a real good shot at me, so I just set there. When shootin' time come, I'd do my share. No use to take the fun away from those anxious folks down there. A couple of more shots from down the ledge, but they done nobody any harm. I took another gulp of coffee and looked out yonder at the mountain peaks. Some of them were fifty, sixty miles off.

I wished I could see the one called the Sleeping Ute, but that mountain was hidden behind the rim yonder.

When I leaned forward to take up the pot, that gent atop the knoll shot right into my fire. I slapped around, putting out sparks. He was going to get almighty annoying if he kept that up.

There were several more shots, but I finished my coffee before I took up my rifle.

Thing about fightin' with folks unused to fightin' is that a body should give them time. They get eager to get on with it and haven't the patience to set and wait. Me, I was in no hurry. I wasn't going no place.

First thing you know they were shootin'—scatterin' lead every which way—but I just set back in my corner enjoying my coffee and let them have at it.

They were wishful that I'd move out where I could shoot back so that gent atop the knoll could settle my hash. I'd no mind to let him do it.

Finally, I just got tired of the racket.

The horses were in the best spot of all. They hadn't picked no fight. I had them in a place where bullets couldn't reach, and they had sense enough to stand there and switch flies off one another.

After a mite I decided that gent on the knoll might be gettin' eager enough to make a fool of himself, so I took my rifle and edged around to where I could peek up yonder without showing too much. Sure enough, I saw his rifle barrel. Then I saw something against the sky—a shoulder in a blue shirt, maybe. It disappeared, but folks being what they are, I just waited, knowing he'd be apt to do the same thing again, and he did.

Me, I just up with that '73 and shot him, right in the whatever it was he was showin'. I heard a yelp, then a rifle fell loose on the grassy slope of that knoll, and I edged out to where I could see down the ledge.

I caught a glimpse of a plaid shirt down thataway. I triggered the '73, and whatever I'd shot at disappeared.

After that there was a kind of letup in the shootin'.

Those shots hadn't stopped them, just made them a mite more cautious. They knew now it wasn't going to be all downhill, but I'm tellin' the world I was a mighty lonesome man, a-settin' there, waitin' for them to come. And only a few miles off I had family tough enough to whip an army. Looked to me like I had it to do all by myself.

Well, that was the way I'd done most things my life long.

I fed a couple of cartridges into my rifle and took a look at the horses. They were standing, half-asleep, undisturbed by the doings of us humans. I went down among them and talked to 'em a little and then eased myself back up to where I'd been.

There was no easy way out of this, but one thing I knew: come nighttime I wasn't going to set waitin'. I was going out among 'em. And I was going shootin'.

Come hell or high water, I was going out yonder. If they wanted to land this fish, they were going to find out they had something on the hook.

CHAPTER XXIV

It was a long day. From time to time a shot came into the hollow, but they made no frontal attack. The failure of the shots from the top of the knoll had apparently left them at a loss, and they hadn't figured out what to do.

Nobody ever won a fight by setting back and waiting, at least, not in my circumstances. In any case, my only way of fighting was to attack, and I believe in it, anyway. Attack, always attack.

They had me bottled up where I couldn't move by day, but night was something else, and I intended to move out and hunt them down. No doubt they planned to come and get me as soon as darkness fell.

Lying there I studied the possible routes out of my cul-de-sac, and getting out was no problem for a man on foot. In my saddlebags I carried my moccasins. I'd been a woodsman before I was ever a rider, and it come natural to me to move quiet.

Many a time as a boy I had either to ease up on game or not get a shot. A kill meant that I'd eat, and often it was only me and the family when pa was gone and the other boys still too young to hunt.

Judging by what Andre had said Pa had come here. Probably he had died here. And he must have had the gold when he reached this place.

What had become of it? Was it still hidden close by?

I set back and took a careful look around. Supposin' I had gold to hide, quite a bit of it. Where would I hide it where it would be unlikely to be found? Supposin' I was here, figured I still had a fightin' chance, but knew I might have to slip out and travel light, just like I was going to do when darkness came?

Where would I hide the gold?

There was a level place of green grass, partly protected from rifle fire by a shoulder of the rock that walled the ledge. There was a sort of cove in the wall, scarcely more than enough to hide the two horses.

A tree that must have fallen five or six years ago lay close by, its trunk breaking up to pay its debt to the soil it came from. Lying near to it was the fallen tree with the brown needles still in place. It must have been broken off this past winter. Those trees hadn't been there when pa made his stand—if he did.

I had another thing to go by. Pa had known all the Indian ways of marking a trail, and he had taught them to us boys. One way was to place one rock atop another as a trail marker and a rock alongside the marker to show the direction of travel. Often when we were youngsters he'd lay out a trail for us to follow. He'd gather a tuft of grass and tie it around with more grass, or he'd break a branch and stick it in the ground to show the way he'd gone.

Often the Indians would bend a living tree to mark the way. From time to time in wandering the woods one will wonder about a tree that grows parallel to the ground for a ways. Chances are it was some marker used by Indians in the long ago.

Pa taught us boys as best he could. He'd find a spot in the deep woods and he'd clear the ground of all leaves, branches, stones, and whatever. Then he'd smooth out the dust, leaving some food, both meat and seeds, in the center. We'd surround it with a circle of branches or stones, and we'd come back each morning to see who'd been there.

It wasn't long until we boys could tell the track of any animal or bird or reptile that crossed the smooth dust.

Pa was forever pointing at some tracks or tree or bunch of rocks and asking us what we thought happened there, or what was happening. It's an amazing thing how much a boy can learn in a short time.

You found where animals had fought, mated, and died. You learned which animals moved about at night, which would come for meat, and which for seeds or other food.

We got so we just saw things without having to look for them. It was natural to us to know what was happening in the mountains and in the forest. Just as people differ one from another, so do the trees, even the trees of one species.

After a while I put my fire together again and fixed a little food, made fresh coffee, and took time to study the situation. Pa had been in this spot twenty years ago, and things would have looked very different. The older of the fallen trees would have been growing then, and several others within the range of my eyes would have been fair-sized trees. Others, larger and older, might now be gone.

The high winds, snows, and ice of the alpine heights are hard on trees. The bristlecone pine, which seems to survive anything, outlasts the others. This shelf where I had taken refuge would be deep under snow much of the year, and when pa was here some snow might have still been left. To understand his situation I had to bring back the shelf the way it must have been when he saw it.

Surely there'd have been snow where I sat, snow in this pocket and along the side where the shadows stayed almost all day long. He'd have made his notch somewhere here, but the tree might have fallen. It might be this very tree that was rotting away before me, or it might have been burned in campfires or fallen clear over the rim. There were scattered carcasses of trees along the steep slope below the cliff.

Pa respected his boys, respected our knowledge of things, and if he'd had the chance he'd have left us a clue, some hint as to where the gold was, and maybe as to what had become of him.

Had the journal ended with the loss of that daybook? Or had he some other means of writing? I'd better consider that.

I needed Orrin here. He had a contemplative mind and he was a lawyer, a man accustomed to dealing with the trickiness of the human mind. Tyrel would have been a help, too, for Tyrel took nothing for granted. He was a right suspicious man. He liked folks, but never expected much of them. If his best friend betrayed him he'd not be surprised. He figured we were all human, all weak at times, and mostly selfish. And we all, he figured, had traits of nobility, self-sacrifice, and courage. In short, we were folks, people.

Tyrel never held it against any man for what he did. He trusted nobody too much, liked most people, and he was wary. But at a time like this he would have been a help. He had a reasoning, logical brain unhampered by much sentiment.

One thing was a help. We Sacketts bred true. I mean, we bred to type. Like the Morgan horse. Pa used to say he'd known a sight of Sacketts one time and another, and they varied in size, but most of them ran to dark, kind of Indian-like features and to willingness to fight. Even those Clinch Mountain Sacketts, who were a cattle-rustling, moonshining lot, would stand fast in a showdown, and they'd never go back on their word or fail a friend.

They might steal his horse, if it was a good one and chance offered, but they were just as like to stand over his wounded body and fight off the redskins or give him one of their own horses, even their only horse, to get away on.

Logan and Nolan, for example. They were Clinch Mountain Sacketts, and their pa was meaner than a rattlesnake in the blind, but they never walked away from a friend in trouble, or anybody else, for that matter.

Nolan was forted up down in the Panhandle country

with some Comanches yonder a-shootin' at him. One of them got lead into him. He nailed that one right through the ears as he turned his head to speak to the other one, and then he wounded the last one. Nolan walked in on him, kicked the gun out of his hand, and stood there looking down at him, gun in his fist, and that Comanche glared right back at him, dared him to shoot, and tried to spit at him.

Nolan laughed, picked that Injun up by the hair and dragged him to his horse. He loaded that Indian on, tied him in place, then mounted his own horse and rode right to that Comanche village.

He walked his horse right in among the lodges and stopped.

The Comanches were fighters. No braver men ever lived, and they wanted Nolan's hair, but they came out and gathered around to see what he had on his mind.

Nolan sat up there in the middle of his mustang, and he told them what a brave man this warrior was, how he had fought him until he was wounded, his gun empty, and then had cussed him and tried to fight him with his hands.

"I did not kill him. He is a brave man. You should be proud to have such a warrior. I brought him back to you to get well from his wounds. Maybe some day we can fight again."

And then he dropped the lead rope and rode right out of that village, walking his horse and never looking back.

Any one of them could have shot him. He knew that. But Indians, of any persuasion, have always respected bravery, and he had given them back one of their own and had promised to fight him again when he had his strength.

So they let Nolan ride away, and to this day in Comanche villages they tell the story. And the Indian he brought back tells it best.

I didn't really have time to contemplate the past. I had mighty little time left and I wanted to find out what happened to pa.

Clouds were making up. Nearly every afternoon there was a brief thundershower high up in the mountains, and now the clouds were gathering. I guess I was feeling kind of pleased about that. I had an idea those folks were new to the high-up hills and if so they were in for a shock.

Rain can fall pretty hard, and of course you're right in the clouds. Right amongst them. Lightning gets to flashing around, and—even without it flashing—the electricity in the air makes your hair prickle like a scared dog's.

I didn't much relish running around atop that mountain with a rifle in my hands, but it looked like I had it to do.

The bulging dark clouds moved down and began to spatter rain, and I came off that log where I was settin' like a chipmunk headin' for a tree. I went around the tree holding my rifle in one hand, scrambled up the rocks, took a quick look, and ran on the double for that knoll.

If they broke and ran for shelter, I would make it. I started up the knoll knowing that in just about a minute it was going to be all wet grass, slippery as ice. Just as I was topping out on the rise a man raised up, rifle in hand.

He'd no idea there was anybody even close. He was getting set to run for shelter from the rain, I figure, and was taking a quick look before he left; and there I was, coming up out of that drifting cloud right at him.

Neither of us had time to think. My Winchester was in my right hand in the trail position, and when he hove up in front of me I just drove the muzzle at him. It was hanging at my side at arm's length. When that man came up off the ground I swang it forward and there was power behind it.

The muzzle caught him right under the nose, smashing up hard. It knocked him right over backwards, and he let a scream out of him like you never heard. It must've hurt real bad.

He tumbled head over heels down the side of that steep knoll and wound up at the bottom, his face all bloody. I stood there looking down at him.

The knoll was kind of like a pyramid too narrow for its height, covered with grass and scattered rocks. That cloud was drifting over, and he could see me up there, rifle in hand.

He figured I was going to kill him, and for a moment there I gave it thought.

"You get off down the mountain, boy," I told him, "and you keep goin'. You folks are about to get me upset."

Still looking at me, he began to back himself off, still lying on the grass, the rain pelting him.

I looked around and there was nobody in sight. I turned and went back down the knoll to my hideout.

When I got to the horses I pulled the picket pins and coiled the ropes. I stowed them away and gathered the reins and was just about to stick a toe in a stirrup when I realized how wet my feet were going to get in those moccasins.

My boots were handy so I got into my slicker and set down to haul on my boots—when my eyes leveled on that crack in the rocks.

It wasn't no kind of a place, just a layered rock where one layer had fallen or been pulled out—leaving a kind of gap not over two inches wide. It was deeper than it looked at first, and there was something in there.

I slipped my hand in and found myself touching some kind of a book. I took it out and it was another day-book, almost like the first, but it was in worse shape.

When I scrambled up that rock wall I must have stepped on a piece of the rock that had been shoved in there to keep the wet off and the animals from gettin' at it.

It was a daybook, and I knew it had been pa's. I shifted it to my left hand and started to slip it into my coat pocket when a voice said, "I'll take that!"

It was Andre Baston, and he was right on the bank with a gun on me.

CHAPTER XXV

There's times when a man might talk himself out of trouble, but this wasn't one of those times.

Andre Baston was a killing man and he had a gun on me. I've known men who would have shot me and taken the book out of my dead hand, but Baston was not only a killer, he was cruel. He liked somebody to know he was going to kill 'em.

Moreover he'd been used to those set-tos where there's a challenge, seconds meet, a duel is arranged, and two men walk out on the greensward—whatever that is—and, after a certain number of paces, they turn around and shoot at each other most politely.

Me, I'd grown up to a different manner of doing. You drew and you shot, and no fancy didoes were cut. Nobody needed to tell me what Andre had in mind. I had the same thing in mind for him only I wasn't wastin' around about it.

He'd said, "I'll take that!" And he had a gun on me.

A man who doesn't want to get shot hadn't better pack a gun in the first place. I knew when I laid my hand on that gun that I was going to get shot, but I also had it in mind to shoot back.

I figured, *all right, he's going to nail me, but if he kills me I'll take him with me, and if he doesn't kill me I'll surely get him.*

He didn't expect it—I had that going for me, but it wasn't enough. My hand went to the gun and she came up fast and smooth. When she came level I was going to let drive, and I kind of braced myself for the shock of a bullet.

My .44 bucked in my hands, and, an instant before it went off, his gun stabbed flame. I just stood there and thumbed back that hammer. *No matter how many times he shoots, you got to kill him,* I told myself. I just eared her back and let 'er bang, and Andre Baston kind of stood up on his toes. I let her go again, and his gun went off into the grass at his feet and he fell off the ledge sidewise and lit right at my feet.

"You!" There was an ugly hatred in his eyes. "You aren't even a *gentleman!*"

"No, sir," I said politely, "but I'm a damned good shot."

Andre Baston, of New Orleans, died on the rim of Cumberland Basin with the rain falling into his wide-open eyes, trickling down his freshly shaved jaws.

"Well, pa," I said, "if this was the one, he's signed the bill for it. You rest easy, wherever you lie."

With a sweep of my palm I swept the water from my saddle and stepped up there on old Ap and pointed his nose down the basin, the buckskin right behind us. We just climbed out of that shelf and rounded a clump of spruce, and I looked back yonder at the knoll, half-hidden in clouds now.

It came to me then, ridin' away, that Andre had missed me. I'd been so almighty sure I was going to get shot, I was ready to take the lead and send it back. But he missed. Maybe when he saw me reaching he hurried too much, maybe the panic came up in him like it does in a lot of men when they know they're going to be shot at—a kind of uncomfortable feeling.

But like I said, when you pick up a weapon you can expect a weapon to be used against you.

They had them a sort of camp on the slope, a mighty poor shelter, I'd say. I rode right up to them, two men I didn't know, and Paul, looking like something blown up against a fence by a wet wind. Of course, Fanny was there, startled to see me, the softness gone from her features, her mouth drawn hard.

"You better go get your uncle," I said. "He's up there lyin' in the rain."

They did not believe me. I had my rifle across my saddlebows, its black muzzle looking one-eyed at them, so they stood quiet.

"Was I in your place," I suggested, "I'd light a shuck for Bourbon Street or places around, and when I got there I'd start burning a few candles at the altar of your Uncle Philip. There's nothing left for you here."

The trail was muddy, full of doubles and switchbacks, with little streams crossing it here and there. That was a day when it kept right on raining, and through the rain dripping off my hat I saw the fresh green of the forest and the grass.

It was a narrow trail, no question of hurrying. All I wanted was to get to the bottom, back down to Shalako where I could wrap myself around a few steaks and some hot coffee. This was a day when I'd rather set by an inside fire and watch the raindrops fall.

Every once in a while when I'd duck under a tree, a few raindrops, always the coldest ones, would shake loose and trickle down the back of my neck.

Alongside the trail, sometimes close by, sometimes down in a rocky gorge below me, was the La Plata. Waterfalls along the trail added to the river's volume. The trail was washed out in places.

Nobody used this trail but the Utes, or occasional hunters and prospectors.

Yet all of a sudden I saw something else. In the bank where the trail passed there was a fresh, scuffed place. My hand went under my slicker to my six-shooter.

Somebody had stepped off this trail minutes before, stepping quickly up into the trees that lined the trail. One boot had crushed the grass on the low bank that edged the trail.

Ap turned quickly around a corner of the trail and I glanced up, seeing nothing. The man had gone into the woods, hearing me on the trail, and he hadn't the time to do more than disappear somewhere just within the edge of the trees.

Who would be coming up here on a day like this? No Indian, for it had been a boot track, a wide boot, not far from new.

Nothing happened. I rode on, switching back and around on the narrow trail, and when I reached a straight stretch I stepped up the pace and let Ap trot for a while.

Safely away, I began now to look for more tracks.

Occasionally I saw them, shapeless, not to be identified, but tracks nonetheless, and the tracks of somebody who did not wish to be seen. Wherever he could, he walked off the trail.

There were places when the sides were too steep, or the gorge beside the trail too deep for him to avoid the trail. The man had a good stride. He was a heavy man, too, but possibly not a tall one despite the good steps he took.

Might be a smaller man carrying a heavy pack. Had the tracks not been so sloppy I might have been able to tell if the man carried a heavy pack or was himself heavy. Of course, it might be both.

It worried me. Who was he? And why was he going up the mountain today?

Well, if he was a friend to the Bastons it did not matter, and if he was their enemy, it might be they'd shoot each other.

I was going for a hot meal, a night's rest, and a chance to put down my gun.

There's something about gold that nags at a man. I've seen it at work a time or two. I think we Sacketts have less of it than most—with us it's land. We like the ownership of land, large pieces of mountain country, that's for us.

Nonetheless, pa labored hard for that gold. He found it, brought it off down the mountain, and now it was cached up yonder . . . sure as shootin' it was there. It puzzled a man to guess where.

By the time I rode up to Shalako the sun was out and sparkling on the rain-wet leaves. Orrin came out of the store and stood waiting.

He gave me a long look. "You all right?"

"I been through it." I stepped down and stood, hands resting on the saddle, and then I turned my head toward him. "I left Andre up yonder. Right where pa was cornered, I think."

"The rest of them?"

"Up there. Paul's there with Fanny and a couple of others."

"Leave your horses," Orrin said. "Judas said to tell

you he'd care for them. You come in and have some grub."

Judas came out to take Ap and the buckskin, and I walked across to the saloon with Orrin.

"There was a man came into town. Had his face all torn up and couldn't talk much, or didn't want to. He went off down the road mumbling to himself."

"He ran into a rifle muzzle, I guess. Orrin, did you see anybody else? Did anybody go up the canyon?"

"Not by daylight. We've been watching. I mean we've been watching that road every minute."

I told him about the tracks in the trail, but he shook his head, having no more explanation than I did.

"Somebody followed pa to that place. Somebody cornered him up there, and he may have been hurt. Pa taught us boys so much, and we've lived about the same. I figured I'd just let myself go the likely way. He left notches here and there, the deep, gashlike blazes, you know." I took the other daybook out of my pocket. "And I found this."

Orrin took it in his hands. "I wonder what pa was thinking, Tell. Why he took to keeping these on that last trip? Do you suppose he had a premonition?"

I'd been thinking of it, too. "Either that, or something was turning wrong with him. He never was much to complain, you know, and we always just took it for granted he was about the strongest man around. Maybe he was feeling poorly and wasn't wishful that we know."

The words were no sooner out than I was sure I'd hit on it. This trip had been pa's last chance to do something for his family. He'd cared for us, but suddenly he might have felt he wouldn't be able to, and he began to worry.

Neither of us wanted to open the book. This would be our last word from pa, and these last few weeks we'd felt close to him again, walking in his footsteps and all. After this we both felt there would be nothing left to the story, nothing but what must have happened when he stopped writing.

Berglund brought some hot soup and bread and I made a meal of it. The book lay there on the table, and from time to time I looked up to see it there.

Tired as I was, my thoughts kept returning to the mountain trail, and I wanted to go back. I wanted to walk there again, to stand on that shelf again looking out over the mountains and sky.

The feeling stayed with me that there was something I had not found.

"Where's Nell Trelawney?" I asked suddenly. "I haven't seen her."

"You will," Orrin chuckled as he said it. "She's been around every day wanting us to go up the canyon and find you. She was sure you were in trouble."

He grinned. "I told her you'd been in trouble all your born days."

"Any more of those Three Eight hands around?"

"Boley McCaire—the young one who was so itchy. He rode into town, but he's been holed up somewhere down the creek. I've a hunch that Baston made some kind of a deal with them."

Something kept worrying me at the back of my mind, and it was not only those tracks along the way. I did not like things left hanging. Nobody went up that mountain trail in the rain without reason. The folks at Shalako had seen nobody pass, and the road was right yonder. Nobody could pass along without being seen, so if somebody had gone up the creek he had taken pains not to be seen.

Who? And why? And what was he doing now?

Judas came in, and then the Tinker. The Tinker sat down near a window where he could watch the street and the trail to the mountains.

"Judas," I said suddenly, "have you known the Bastons long?"

He hesitated and seemed to be considering. "Fifty years," he said quietly. "Possibly even longer."

"Would Andre have followed Pierre and stabbed him?"

Judas thought for a moment. "Of course. But I do not believe he did. It was someone else."

"Who?"

He shrugged, and then he said, "Andre would not have dared let Pierre live, not after attacking him. The very idea would have been frightening. Had Andre any thought that Pierre lived after he shot him, he'd have killed him or fled—to Africa or South America."

"Why, in God's name?"

"Andre was afraid. He was a brave man, although a murderer, but he feared one man. He was afraid of Philip."

"*Afraid* of him?"

Judas looked at me, then at the rest of us. "Yes, you see Philip was the worst of them, by far the worst."

CHAPTER XXVI

We looked at him, wondering if he was joking, but he was very serious.

"I knew him, you see, and he was good to us. I mean to his slaves, but we had no choice but to obey him, and, being wise, we did obey.

"He liked Pierre Bontemps. He was also amused by him. Pierre was a romantic, an adventurer. Both men had been buccaneers, and this was known of Pierre, but not of Philip.

"Philip surrounded himself with calm, dignity, and reserve. He liked me because I had some education and because he knew I did not talk of what I knew or had seen.

"He was not a vindictive man, not a hater. He was simply a man without scruple. He had contempt for others, whom he considered less than himself. He did nothing to exhibit himself except in that quiet, dignified manner.

"He removed anyone who got in his way. Had you not killed Andre, he would have had it done, or done it himself, for Andre had become notorious.

"Each of us has in his mind an image of what he believes himself to be, and Philip Baston saw himself as a prince of the old school. He had read Machiavelli, studied the careers of Orsini, Sforza, and Sigismondo Malatesta, and in his small way he lived accordingly.

"The Bastons had money, and, from time to time,

power, but not enough of either to please any of them. Philip served briefly at sea in a French ship, then became a pirate.

"Lafitte was notorious. Baston was more cunning. He slipped into New Orleans and bought property, always small pieces, nothing to attract attention. He bought land in other parts of Louisiana, and when it became no longer safe to carry on as a pirate he simply came ashore, moved into the old Baston home and carried on as if he had never been gone. It wasn't realized for several years that he was enormously wealthy.

"He aspired to be governor. He lived in the grand manner, and anyone who got in his way was removed. Now he thinks of his family, his name. At first he looked on Andre's duels with favor. They had a certain style, and it was good to be feared. There came a time however when it became obvious that Andre *killed*. He was not content to win. This was looked upon with distaste, and I believe that for some time Philip has intended to be rid of Andre."

"But you said Andre was afraid of him. Is Philip such a fighter?"

"He is a superb swordsman and a dead shot, but Philip would not have done it himself unless forced into the position. He would have made other arrangements."

It was interesting, but nothing that meant much to us now. Philip Baston was in New Orleans.

What interested me more was the identity of the unknown man who left the footprints on the trail.

If he had a horse, where had it been?

Orrin got up. "You better get some rest. I am going to ride over and see Flagan."

The Swede had a back room with a spare bunk in it, and he showed me to the place. I shucked my boots, hat, and gun belt and stretched out on that bunk with a deep sigh. I'd no recollection of ever feeling so tired before.

I'd been on the trail for a long while, and a man tires faster when his nerves are on edge. When you're hunting and being hunted, every fiber of your being is poised and ready.

I felt the tenseness go out of me slow, and I dozed off. I woke briefly and watched the aspens beyond the window. It was fifty or sixty feet to the edge of the woods. The curtain stirred in the breeze, and I watched it lazily, then drifted off into a sound sleep.

Under the aspens the man waited. He had a shotgun in his hands, and he knew what he wanted to do. Inside the room near the opposite wall was a chair. Over the back of the chair hung a gun belt.

He heard the boots hit the floor and thought he heard a creak of a bed when the man lay down.

Just a few minutes now . . . a few minutes.

The big, good-looking brother had ridden off on his horse. The Negro was in the barn, working on some of their saddlegear. The Tinker had taken a pole and headed for the La Plata, and Swede Berglund was tending that garden he was trying. So William Tell Sackett was there alone, and soon he would be asleep.

The hunter had patience. He had seen the young Sackett with another daybook in his hands, but the daybook could not have been with the body. He had gone over it thoroughly those twenty years ago.

Was it with the gold? No . . . for gold hadn't been brought off the mountain today.

The book would certainly tell where old man Sackett had hidden the gold. They had all been so sure Sackett was dead, and Pierre, too. Well, Pierre was dead now, that was sure, and so was Sackett.

The trouble was Sackett had gone back and gotten the gold after they were all gone. Not all the gold on Treasure Mountain, but a good lot of it, anyway.

This William Tell Sackett worried him. The man was a tracker, and a good one. He could read sign like an Apache, and there was no safety with him about.

Sackett had killed Andre. The man had not seen it but he heard the girl and the others talking of it. That must have taken some doing, for Andre was dangerous, good with a gun, and ready to use it.

So much the better. With Andre gone, the rest of them were nothing. Paul was a weakling. That girl was murderous enough, but she was a woman, and she was too impulsive.

Well inside the curtain of aspens, crouched low among the tall grass, wild flowers, and oak brush, he was well hidden. He would give Sackett plenty of time to get to sleep, really to sleep.

Crouched in the bushes, the man waited. The shotgun had two barrels, and he wore a long-barreled six-shooter for insurance and had a rifle on his horse. As he waited he once more studied the ground. He knew just where each foot would touch ground, where he would go into the trees, where he would turn after entering the woods. He had chosen two alternative routes. He was a careful man.

Ten to fifteen seconds to the window, lean in, fire his shot. Then, instead of running directly away, he would run along the wall of the saloon, go around the outhouse, and crouch along the corral into the scrub oaks.

On the other side of the oak brush a trail dipped into the river bottom where his horse waited. He would ride south, away from the canyon, where there was more room to lose himself.

He waited a moment longer, got to his feet, glanced left and right, and stepped out of the brush, walking swiftly to the window.

Glancing left and right, he saw no one. The shotgun came up in his hands, and he was almost running when he reached the window. He started to thrust the shotgun into the open window when suddenly a voice on his left said, "You lookin' for something, mister?"

It was that Trelawney girl, and she had a rifle in her hands, not aimed at him, but in a position where only an instant would be needed to aim it.

He hesitated, kept his head tilted downward. He muttered under his breath, then turned sharply away and walked toward the outhouse.

"Mister? *Mister!*"

He ducked around the small building and ran along the corral into the woods. Another ten seconds! He swore, bitterly. Another ten seconds and he would have killed Tell Sackett and be on the run . . . well away to his horse.

Nell walked to the window, glancing in. Taking one more quick look after the fleeing man, gone now, she went around to the front. The Tinker was standing in front of the store. She explained quickly.

The Tinker glanced toward the woods beyond the corral. "He's gone. You scared him off."

"But who *was* he? I never saw him before!"

The Tinker shrugged. "It will not happen again." He walked around the building, glanced toward the woods, then sat down. "I'll stay right here until he wakes up. Don't you worry now."

Morning light was laying across the windowsill before my eyes opened, and for a time I just lay still, letting myself get wide awake. That there was the soundest sleep I'd had in a long, long time. Finally, I swung my feet to the floor and reached for my boots.

Something stirred outside the window, and Tinker said, "Tell? Better come out and have a look."

When I was dressed and out there beside him, he showed me the tracks. There were only parts of two foot tracks, the rest were on grass and left no mark that remained to show size.

It was the same track I'd seen on the trail.

"He was out to get you, Tell. There's a place where he waited in the aspens over there. He must've waited an hour or more."

In the earth back of the outhouse we found another track, smudged and shapeless because he had been running. We found where his horse had stood, tied and waiting.

I studied the tracks, knowing I had seen them before, but without remembering where. To a tracker a track is like a signature, and as easy to identify, but this was not one I had remembered, hence it was no one I had ever followed. It was simply a track I had noted casually without paying it any mind, but one thing I knew. If I saw that track again, I would remember it.

Orrin came in from the ranch. "Good place," he said, "and I've found a spot for us."

When I told him what had happened, he looked

grim. "I should have come back. I knew I should have come back."

"Nothing gets by that girl," Tinker commented. "She had that man dead to rights."

We drank coffee, ate breakfast, and watched the cloud shadows change on Baldy. "I'm going up there again," I said. "I've got to settle it in my mind. I've got find what remains of him."

"He's lost," Berglund said. "Coyotes or bears carried off the bones . . . or the buzzards dropped them. Nothing lasts long up there that isn't stone."

"There's evidence of that," the Tinker said quietly, "coming down the trail."

Four horses, four riders—a rain-wet, beat-up looking crew—and one of them was Fanny Baston. Paul was there, one hand all tied up with a bandage, and those two riders they'd picked up from somewhere.

They came down the trail, and we stepped outside to see them pass, but they looked neither to the right nor the left, they just rode on through. They carried nothing, nor did they stop for grub.

"She's a beautiful woman," Orrin said. "You should have seen her the night we met."

"Mountains are hard upon evil," I said. "They don't hold with it."

Back inside we drank coffee whilst Judas saddled up for us. He came across the road, a neat black man in a neat black coat. "I would like to ride along with you, suh," he suggested.

"Why not? You're a man to ride with, Priest. But ride ready for war. It may come upon us."

We packed the buckskin again, for we'd be gone one night, anyway.

We rode out into the street and started for the trail, and two more riders came up from the other end of town. It was Nell Trelawney and old Jack Ben.

"See here," I said, pulling rein, "this is a rough ride, and you've been ailin'."

"I ain't ailin' now," old Jack Ben said irritably, "and as for rough rides, I was ridin' rough country before your head was as high as a stirrup! You just ride along now, and pay us no mind."

"No use to argue," Orrin said. "He was always a hard-headed, unreasonable old coot."

Jack Ben snorted, but when we started off they were right behind us, and there they stayed, all the way up the mountain, and we rode with our rifles ready to hand. Yet no trouble came to us, and we rode easy in our saddles, the wind cool and pleasant in our faces, winding around and doubling back, the wild waters of the La Plata tumbling over the rocks or slowing down where the canyon widened out.

Midday was long gone when we rode into the basin. The grass was a glorious green, wild flowers were everywhere.

When we went down on the shelf Andre's body was gone. I showed them where the daybook had been. We had brought it along to read on the spot.

It was getting on for sundown, so we unsaddled and staked out our horses. When the fire was lit and the coffee on, I took out the daybook.

CHAPTER XXVII

Judas was fixing supper. The Tinker sat a little away from us in the dark where he could listen better to the night sounds.

With firelight flickering on the faces around, I tilted the book to catch the glow and settled down to read. There was a smudge on the first page.

. . . wind blowing, hard to write. Played out. A man trailin' me got a bullet into me when I went to move the picket pin. Low down on my left side. Hurts like hell. Lost blood. Worst is, he's in a place where I can't get a shot at him. Dasn't have no fire.

Later: shot twice. Missed. I shot at sound, figured to make him carefuller. Gold hid. Got to hide this book—the other one's been stolen. If the boys come a-huntin', soon or late they'll find it. I trust if somebody else does he'll call the boys and share up. I don't expect no man to find gold and give it all up. Figured that was Andre, yonder. It ain't. Andre ain't that good in the brush. This'ns like Injun.

Later: ain't et for two days. Canteen empty. Licked dew off the grass. Caught a swallow of rain in my coffee-pot. Wounds in bad shape.

Writing time to time. Boys will find that gold. They'll remember when it comes right down to it. That Orrin, he should recall, him always wantin' the cream of things. No further than from the house to the old well. Ma could find it. How many times she scolded that boy!

Comin'. Been backed up here five days now. Grub's gone. Coffee's gone. No water but dew and rain. Whoever it is out there won't take a chance. Got a funny walk. Hear him. Got another bullet into me. Boys, I ain't goin' to make it. Be good boys. Be good. Take care—got to put this away.

He was cornered like an old bear driven to the wall, wounded and dying, but his last thoughts were of us. He'd have handled everything all right if he could have moved around, but he was bad hurt. That bullet in the side, now. That must have been worse than he said . . . and no water. He must have caught some rain in his coffeepot, but that wouldn't have been much. He would have been slower in his movements with that bruised hipbone.

When I finished reading, we just sat there thinking of pa, remembering the way he walked, the lessons he taught us, his humor, his handiness with tools.

"That gold's somewheres about," Jack Ben said, "an' he left you clues. 'No further than from the house to the old well.' That there should mean somethin'. I recall that old well. She always had good water. Cold water, too. On'y it was too far from the house on a winter's mornin' so your grandpa dug one closer."

"It ain't the gold, Jack Ben. It's pa. We want to find what remains of him."

"You know what I think?" The Tinker turned his head toward us, firelight glinting on the gold rings in his ears. "I think that's the same man after you. The one who killed your pa. I think he's out there right now."

We set quiet, contemplating on that. It could be . . . but who?

"A Higgins," Jack Ben said, remembering the old feud in Tennessee. "It must be a Higgins you've paid no mind to. He got your pa, now he's after the rest of the Sacketts."

That might be, but something worried me. Couldn't put a finger on it, but something about this whole setup bothered me to fits. Nell set over there kind of watching me and that upset my considering. Hard to keep a mind on business with her setting over there breathing. Every time she took a deep breath my forehead broke out with sweat.

"Go back over it," Judas suggested. "Cover every step. Possibly there is a thing that does not fit, something that will explain it all."

"It might be the McCaire outfit," Orrin said. "Charley McCaire didn't take kindly to losing those horses even if he had no hand in stealing them."

"You don't think he did?" I asked.

"I doubt it. I think it was somebody in his outfit. But once he had them he didn't want to give them up or to have it believed that anyone in his outfit was a thief. If Tyrel hadn't ridden up when he did we'd have had to shoot our way out."

"I don't think it's any of them," I said. "There's something odd about this man."

"What became of Swan?" Judas asked.

I shrugged. I'd been wondering that myself. We'd seen nothing of him, yet surely he was around. He was not with Paul and Fanny when they left . . . if they had.

Finishing my coffee, I threw the grounds into the fire and rinsed out my cup. We would find the gold. I was sure of that, but I had never been a money-hungry man. We'd started out to find pa, or what remained of him, and we'd come a long way. We had to find out what happened in those last hours or minutes.

I put my cup away and went into the darkness near the trees, stood there a moment, and worked my way over to where the Tinker was.

He spoke as I neared him. "Tell? There's somebody or something out there."

His whisper was very soft, only for my ears. I squatted near him. "Nothing definite . . . just something moving . . . scarcely no sound."

I noticed that he held his knife in his hand. The Tinker was always a careful man.

"I'm going out there."

"No." The Tinker put his hand on my arm. "I will go."

"This here's my job. Just tell them I am out there. And be careful, there's no telling what he will do."

It was very dark. There were a few stars among scattered clouds. I made no attempt to keep to the brush. I moved through the knee-high grass and wild flowers.

When I was thirty yards out from camp, I stopped to listen. What was he doing? Trying for a shot? Or merely listening?

I moved on among the scattered spruce, keeping low to the ground. I stopped, and a voice spoke, very low.

"Have you found the gold?"

There was a chill along my back. "No," I said after a moment.

"It is mine. It is all mine. You will not find it."

That voice! There was something . . . some thread of sound . . .

"We can find it," I said calmly, "and no one else can. The message my father left is one only we could understand."

There was a long silence. "I do not believe it. How could that be?"

"It has to do with our home in Tennessee."

What manner of man was this who would so coolly talk to me in the darkness? And where was he? The direction was obvious, but if I leaped, and missed, I'd be dead in the next moment.

"It is *my* gold." He spoke softly. "Go away and I'll not kill you."

"You're through killing. If anybody does it now, it will be us."

He did not speak, and I wondered if he were gone. I listened . . . the man was a ghost in the woods. I was good, but this man, I believed, was better.

"You killed my father," I said.

"He was a good man. I did not wish to do it, but he had my gold."

"The Frenchmen mined the gold. They buried it. They sold their claim to it with Louisiana. It was anybody's gold."

"You will not have it. I will kill you all."

After a moment of listening, I said, "Where is my father's body?"

If I could keep him talking, just a little longer. I shifted my position slightly, making no sound.

"It is beyond there, beyond your camp. I buried him in a crack. It is at the edge, near the roots of a tree."

The faintest sound. I moved swiftly, felt the sudden rush of a body in the darkness, saw the gleam of a knife in a short, wicked sidewise swing at my ribs. He swung with his right arm, and I pulled back and dropped to my right. His knife went past me, and I rolled up on the small of my back and kicked out viciously with both feet, kicking where his body had to be.

The double kick caught him on the side and knocked him rolling. Coming up like a cat, knife in hand, I went for him. I saw the black bulk of him roll up and come at me, felt the edge of the knife and the point take my sleeve, and then I came up on his right side and brought my knife up from below.

His elbow caught my wrist and I almost lost my grip on the knife. He twisted away, turned, and threw his weight into me. He was heavy and bull-strong. The charge threw me back, but I caught my left forearm under his chin and brought him over with me. He landed on his back just above me and then we both came up, panting fiercely, gasping for breath at that altitude.

He circled . . . I could barely see him. I could hear his breath and see the cold light gleam along his blade. Suddenly I stopped, poised, yet still. Instantly he threw himself into me and I sidestepped off to my left, leaving my extended right leg for him to trip over. As his toe hooked over my leg, I swung back and down with my blade.

It caught him—too high—it ripped his coat and must

have nicked his neck, for I heard a gasp of pain and then he wheeled into me again. This time his head was up and I jabbed him in the face with my fist. He did not expect it; my fist smashed him back on his heels, and I stepped in, stabbing low and hard.

At the last instant he tried to evade my thrust, throwing himself backward down a small declivity. For an instant he vanished, and then I was down and after him.

He was gone.

Stopping, poised for battle, I listened. Not a sound except a soft wind in the trees. A cloud drifted over the stars and it was darker. Every sense alert, I listened.

Nothing . . . nothing at all.

A brief, utterly futile battle. A moment of desperate struggle, and then nothing.

Yet I should have known. He was a sure-thing killer, who could stab the wounded and helpless Pierre, who could shoot my father from ambush and then lurk, waiting for days for a final shot.

He had thought to kill me there in the darkness, coming at me suddenly, yet I had been ready. And I had nicked him. Of that I was sure.

After a moment I walked back. "I believe I scratched him," I said and explained.

At the edge of the cliff where he had said my father's body was hidden, I hesitated. It was the very edge, and there looked to have been some crumbling. Probably the result of the tree roots.

There was a crack, all right, and some dirt had been filled in. Orrin came closer, holding a burning branch in his left hand. I leaned over to look closer, put my foot on the outer edge of the crack and leaned still further, astride the crack.

Suddenly there was a grating sound, the outer edge fell away under my foot and I felt myself falling. Half-turning I made a futile grab at anything, the rock crumbling from under my feet.

A hand caught mine, the branch dropped, another hand grabbed my sleeve, and I was hauled up on the ledge.

There was a moment when I said nothing. I looked

over into the terrible void of blackness behind me, listening to the last particles of rock fall, strike, and rattle away on the last slope.

"Thanks," I said.

"It was a trap," Orrin said dryly. "There's more than one way to kill a man."

CHAPTER XXVIII

We still had no idea who the killer was. He was somebody who fancied he'd a claim on all that gold, and he was bound and determined to keep everybody else away and to have it all for himself.

At daylight we took a look at the place where I'd almost gone over. There was no evidence to show that a body had ever been there. I reckon the killer had seen the place, figured it was ready to collapse, and just used it on chance.

A woodsman is forever noticing small things like that. He'll have in his mind many possible camps that he'll never have time to use, and he'll notice tangles to avoid, things a man might trip over, and bad footing generally. After a time a man takes all these things in without really thinking about it. But if something is out of place he will see it instantly.

Judas fixed us bacon and eggs from the outfit he'd brought up the trail. It wasn't often we had eggs unless setting down at table, but Judas was a planning man, and he'd packed for good cooking. When we finished I took my Winchester, shifted into moccasins, and walked out to where we'd had our scuffle the night before.

There were tracks aplenty, but might few of them a body could read, for we'd fought mostly on crushed-down grass and flowers, and some of them were already springing back into place.

After a while I found a couple of fair prints. It was the same boot I'd seen on the trail, and I worked around, trying to pick up sign that would take me where he was going.

Trailing a man like that would be like trailing an old silvertip grizzly. He'd be watching his back trail and would be apt to see me before I saw him, and that wasn't pleasant to contemplate.

Not that I had anybody to mourn much for me but brothers. Ange was dead, the other girls I'd known were scattered and gone, but I could do some mourning for myself. It seemed to me I had a lot of living to do and no particular desire to cash in my chips up here in Cumberland Basin.

Nevertheless, I poked around. He'd taken off in an almighty hurry, not scared, mind you, but lacking that extra percentage he always had to have. When he took those first steps he'd be getting away, not thinking of hiding a trail. By his third or fourth step he'd be thinking of that, if I knew my man.

Sure enough, I found a toe print, gouged deep. I followed a few bruised blades of grass, the edge of a heel print, a crushed pine cone, and a slip in a muddy place, and I came through a patch of scattered spruce and into the open beyond.

I had to pull up short. Chances were nine out of ten he'd changed direction right there. So I scouted around and after a few minutes worked out a trail down into the hollow that lay on the east side of the basin. He had gone down into it, then switched on a fallen log, walked its length, and started back up to the ridge.

By night he couldn't see what he'd done, but crushed grass or leaves had left a greenish smudge atop that log in two places. He had stepped on the log and grass from his boots had stuck it, just as a body will track dirt and the like into a house.

Four or five places in the next hundred yards or so took me along a diagonal route to the high-line trail. That Ghost Trail, as some called it.

A pebble kicked from its place on the muddy path and a couple of partial tracks showed me he was following along the trail.

This here was rifle country, most of it wide open, for the trees give out in the high-up country. Trees were scattered hither and yon, singly or in bunches, among some brush. Higher up the only trees had been barbered by the wind until they looked like upturned brushes. Then there was grass and bare rock, the far-away mountains on every hand, and over all the sky, always scattered with white clouds.

If that hidin' man was in a swivet to get himself killed he'd have to bring it to me. Generally speaking I'm not a techous man, taking most things calm. When a man is about to get shot at he'd better be calm. As much as he can be, at least. Nobody looks favorably on the idea of being shot at.

Trouble was, it was such all-fired pretty country, a man had trouble keeping his mind to it. And quiet? No sound but maybe an eagle, some distance off.

You'd think that in a bald out country like that there'd be no place to hide, but there were places, and any one of them might hide that man.

He'd held to the path—a wise man holds to what trails he can find in the mountains. I picked up sign here and there. He'd slowed down, and a couple of times he'd stopped to catch breath or to ponder.

He knew come daybreak I'd be seekin' his sign. I never minced about shootin' when it had come to that. Back in the Tennessee hills nobody did. Many a girl back yonder bloused her waist to carry a pistol, and we Sackett boys had been toting shootin' irons since we were as tall as pa's belt.

A man walked wary facin' up to a man like this one, so I held my rifle in two hands and kept it right up there where I could shoot without wasting time.

The trail led past a couple of small pools of water, then took a sharp right-hand switch to go out along the ridge toward the north. Spread out before me was a sight of beautiful country that I knowed nothing about but tell-of.

Folks around had talked of it. I'd heard some talk from Cap Rountree when we were up on the Vallecitos that time, and from others here and there. I was looking down Magnetic Gulch toward Bear Creek, and the bear-toothed mountains opposite were Sharkstooth Peak, Banded Mountain, and beyond it the peak of Hesperus.

From where I stood she dropped off some two thousand feet to the bottoms along Bear Creek. I was twelve thousand feet up. I hunkered down behind some rocks, sort of sizing things up before I moved out.

An eagle soared yonder toward the Sharkstooth, and as I looked, some elk came out of the trees into open country and moved across a bench toward the north of the gulch. Now something had moved those elk . . . they weren't just a-playin' "Skip to My Lou." They hied themselves across the clearin' and into the trees.

Might be a bear or a lion, they grow them big in these hills, especially the grizzlies. The grizzly was big, and, when riled, he was mean, but he wouldn't last—because he was fearless. Until the white man came along with his rifle-guns the grizzly was king of the world. He walked where he had a mind to, and nobody trifled with his temper. He couldn't get used to man, although lately he'd become cautious. Maybe too late.

The ridge trail led along the west side of the mountain along here. A man with a rifle would have to be a good shot, used to mountain country.

I stood up and went down into the trees just north of the gulch. When I got into the trees I hunkered down and listened.

There was only the wind, the eternal wind, moving along the high-up peaks, liking them as much as we did.

The grass smelled good. I looked at the rough, gray bark of an old tree, peeling a mite here and there. I saw where a pika had been feeding, and I looked off down the sunlit slope and saw nothing. Then I turned toward the dark clump of spruce further down the slope. I felt suddenly hungry and I stood up and put my left hand into my pocket for some jerky.

I put my rifle down against a limb and boosted the bottom of the pocket a little to get at the jerky. And then from behind me I heard that voice. "Got you, Sackett! Turn around and die!"

Well, I didn't figure he meant to sing me no lullabies, nor the words to "Darlin' Cory," so when I turned around my hand was movin' and I hauled out that ol' .44, eared her back and let 'er bang.

He had a rifle and when I turned I was lookin' right down the barrel. I just said to myself, Tell Sackett, you'll die like your pa done, lonesomelike and hunted down. But that .44 was a pretty good gun. She knew her piece and she spoke it, clear and sharp. I felt the *whiff* of his bullet.

He'd missed. The best of us do it, but a body hadn't better do so when the chips are down and you've laid out your hand on the table with no way but to win or die.

My bullet took him. It took him right where he lives, and the second one done the same like it wanted company.

He couldn't believe he could miss. Maybe he was too sure of it. I stood there, a long, tall man from the Tennessee hills with my pistol in my fist, and I watched him go.

He wanted to shoot again, but that first shot had done something to him, cut his spinal cord, maybe, for his hands kind of opened up and the rifle slid into the grass.

"Nativity Pettigrew," I said, "where did you bury pa?"

His voice was hoarse. "There's a green hillside where a creek runs down at the base of Banded Mountain. You'll find him there at the foot of a rock, a finger that points at the sky, and if you look sharp you'll find his grave and the marker I carved with my hands.

"He had my gold and he had to die, but there's no gainsaying he tried . . . I liked him, lad, but I shot him dead and buried him there where he fell.

"Beat as he was, and wounded bad, he crawled over the mountain to get me. It was him or me, there at the last, and I carry the lead he gave me."

He lay there dying, his eyes open wide to the sun, and I hated him not. He'd played a rough game and, when the last cards were laid down, he lost. But it might have been me.

"When we get the gold out, I'll give some to your wife. She's a good woman," I told him.

"Please," he said.

He died there, and I'd bury him where he fell.

When I came up to the campfire, they were sitting

around and waiting. Flagan was there, who'd come up from Shalako, riding a mouse-colored horse.

"You'll have to forget Hippo Swan," Orrin said. "He came hunting you to Shalako, and Flagan said you weren't the only Sackett, and they fought."

"Sorry, Tell," Flagan said, "but he'd come wanting and I'd not see him go the same way. He fought well but his skin cut too easy, and now he's gone down the road feelin' bad."

"We found the gold, too," Orrin said. "Remember what pa said about me always wanting the cream of things and about the distance to the old well and how many times ma scolded me for it.

"Well, I got to thinking. That word *cream* did it. Remember how we used the well to keep our milk cold? When I was a youngster I used to go out and skim the cream off. Ma was always after me about it. Well, this was the same kind of place—a hole in the rocks— about the same distance away as the well.

"He'd laid rocks back into the hole, threw dirt and such at it, I guess. Anyway, we pulled out the stones and there she was. More than enough to buy us land and cattle to match Tyrel's."

I sat there, saying nothing, and they all looked at me. Then Orrin said, "What happened to you?"

"It was Nativity Pettigrew," I said. "Not so crippled up as he made out. Pa followed him—maybe a mile out there, or more. He crawled up on him and they swapped shots. Pa got lead into him but pa was killed. and Nativity buried him yonder on the slope of Banded Mountain."

"Kind of him," Orrin said, and I agreed.

"We'll do the same for him," I said. "Where he lies we'll put him down. What was it pa used to say? 'Where the chips fall, there let them lie.' "

Nell Trelawney stood up. "Are you going home now, Tell? It's time."

"I reckon," I said, and we went to our horses together.

ABOUT THE AUTHOR

LOUIS L'AMOUR, born Louis Dearborn L'Amour, is of French-Irish descent. Although Mr. L'Amour claims his writing began as a "spur-of-the-moment thing," prompted by friends who relished his verbal tales of the West, he comes by his talent honestly. A frontiersman by heritage (his grandfather was scalped by the Sioux), and a universal man by experience, Louis L'Amour lives the life of his fictional heroes. Since leaving his native Jamestown, North Dakota, at the age of fifteen, he's been a longshoreman, lumberjack, elephant handler, hay shocker, flume builder, fruit picker, and an officer on tank destroyers during World War II. And he's written four hundred short stories and over fifty books (including a volume of poetry).

Mr. L'Amour has lectured widely, traveled the West thoroughly, studied archaeology, compiled biographies of over one thousand Western gunfighters, and read prodigiously (his library holds more than two thousand volumes). And he's watched thirty-one of his westerns as movies. He's circled the world on a freighter, mined in the West, sailed a dhow on the Red Sea, been shipwrecked in the West Indies, stranded in the Mojave Desert. He's won fifty-one of fifty-nine fights as a professional boxer and pinch-hit for Dorothy Kilgallen when she was on vacation from her column. Since 1816, thirty-three members of his family have been writers. And, he says, "I could sit in the middle of Sunset Boulevard and write with my typewriter on my knees; temperamental I am not."

Mr. L'Amour is re-creating an 1865 Western town, christened Shalako, where the borders of Utah, Arizona, New Mexico, and Colorado meet. Historically authentic from whistle to well, it will be a live, operating town, as well as a movie location and tourist attraction.

Mr. L'Amour now lives in Los Angeles with his wife Kathy, who helps with the enormous amount of research he does for his books. Soon, Mr. L'Amour hopes, the children (Beau and Angelique) will be helping too.